Tresaith Asylum

By

A A Prideaux

A CIP catalogue record for this title is

Available from the British Library.

ISBN 978-09930676-8-6

www.paganuspublishing.co.uk

First Published in 2016

Paganus Publishing

Ruthin

Denbighshire

Paganus Publishing

Cover Designed by Richard Prideaux © 2016

DEDICATION

This book is dedicated to all the horses and dogs I own or have ever owned.

They keep me sane.

STORY DESCRIPTION.

Tresaith Asylum has been closed for many years but the strange sights and noises heard and seen along the empty, dark corridors constantly attract ghost hunters to trespass and investigate. When the police become involved following a possible murder in the grounds, the terrifying truth of the Asylum and its hidden secrets are revealed.

DI Revie and his team endeavour to explain the extraordinary supernatural events which will eventually change all of their lives.

Please do note that any similarities between people living or dead are entirely coincidental. This is a work of fiction and is meant to offend exactly – no one.

AUTHOR

A A Prideaux is a businesswoman and an author. She has horses and dogs and lives in Wales.

CONTENTS

CHAPTER ONE

The Townsend family had lived in the Welsh village of Tresaith all of their lives.

Although perhaps that was not strictly true as 10 year old Roy Townsend and his family had been evacuated from Manchester to Tresaith during the war where they were forced to live in one of the Nissan huts on the outskirts of the town. After hostilities ceased, Mother Townsend refused to go back to Manchester to join her drunken and abusive husband and so the young family continued to squat in the huts with a few other families until the local council were forced to place them in the new council houses being built nearby. Roy wooed and married a girl called Betty Gregory, who although living in a farmworker's cottage alongside her eight siblings, was considered upmarket for Roy. Betty's mother did not approve of the match, but was powerless to prevent her now 21 year old daughter from doing as she pleased.

Although he had not seen his father since they left Manchester in 1940 and could not have been influenced by him, Roy became a drunken, philandering and uneducated young man, who resented the better-offs in Tresaith and would cheat or rob from them whenever he could. Just like his dad.

Blonde and blue eyed, the young Roy was very attractive to the opposite sex and revered and admired by his male peers. Even though his family lived in extreme poverty, his charming and criminal ways somehow gave him more kudos.

Roy was introduced to sex and local girls quite early on in his life. His most memorable event, which he relished in telling people for years afterwards, was when his friend had gone up Love Lane. He had taken his girlfriend to 'dress her belly' and told the young Roy to keep watch. Within minutes the girl's mother appeared and began to stride up the lane.

"Seen our girl?" she asked.

"Yes," Roy answered, "Do you want me to fetch her?"

"Naa, love, I have an idea what she's up to and want to catch her at it." She carried on striding.

Roy jumped the field gate in one, ran along the hedge and appeared at a further gate where he saw Bill on top of his latest and both of them had their knickers around their ankles.

He bent down and slapped his friend on his shoulder and shouted, "Get off, her mother's coming!"
Bill did as he was told and with trousers in one hand he jumped the nearby gate into the field. They scarpered down the hill and were soon running back into the Town. Mother had rounded a bend in the lane and seen her bewildered daughter lying on the ground, dress up,

knickers down and no one else around. She received good belting from her mum but came up with no better explanation other than she thought she may have fainted in the heat.

As he got older, Roy fucked all the village girls who were available, three of Betty's sisters being amongst them. It could not be said that he had deflowered them. The girls of this town, of many towns back then were free and easy and married only when they really had to. That was what happened with Betty. She got pregnant, deciding that Roy would be her ideal husband and encouraged her father to encourage Roy. Roy for his part found Betty mildly attractive, easily malleable and unlikely to complain too loudly about him doing as he pleased. So he married her. He had sex with her sister Maggie against the wall of the outside toilets during the reception at the local pub, 'The Dog'. Betty did not know, she may have guessed, but she did not know. She spent her entire married life never really knowing what Roy was doing. He always came home to her, so in the end, it didn't really matter.

Roy had plenty of ideas that would make their family rich. Betty worked as a cleaner at Tresaith manor house and Mrs Tresaith allowed Betty to remain almost up to her due date and come back again a week or so later. Roy allowed her to work there too and arranged for her sister Joan to babysit the four children while Betty worked. He paid Joan in nights out and sex and even persuaded Joan to do the ironing and some baking. Joan told her husband she did it to help out poor Betty and she told Betty that she enjoyed the job.

By the time Roy had bought two fish and chip vans, Betty was able to work on those during the evenings too. Sister Maggie had to be brought in and she demanded cash in addition to the sex. Roy obliged and Betty was just too tired to enquire about what was really going on.

Roy had also roped in Joan's husband in the purchasing of a large digger which they used on building sites and local farms. Most of the work was dealt with in cash and Bill Gittins was never included in the negotiations. When the business finally went bust, Roy had been able to buy a house in the centre of the town while Bill had re-mortgaged his own and gone back to the dairy to work.

They kept the fish and chip vans and Betty now had her name on all things financial. Roy was no longer allowed to hold any accounts. But Betty had no more influence than she had previously for she was still under the controlling influence of her determined and bullying husband. Documents and cheque books were put under her nose and she was told to sign. It meant that Roy became craftier in his dealings and his cash receipts. Roy could scarcely read nor write and so through his arrogance and controlling ways he tried to override his reliance on stupid women in order to cover this failing.

There was a garage in the village with a small showroom and yard at the rear. The owner, Richard

Fawkes wanted to retire and confided in Roy one night in The Dog.

"I really want to sell the place, but my great-grandparents bought the place yonks ago and I feel a bit guilty."

"I don't know why you should. They only got it to keep the carts and the horses they rented out, your Dad changed it to cars and you carried on. But you don't have to keep carrying on."

"I know I don't, but it would be horrible to see it get into the hands of strangers," mused Richard.

"I've got an idea! You stay in the house and let me rent the yard and garage! That way you get to keep it, but it is still in use!"

Drunken Richard said, "But could you afford it? And what about the cars and all the stock in the storeroom?"

Quick thinking Roy answered, "Well, I could pay those off every week. I can afford it, if not officially, then I've always got plenty of cash. We could draw something up now, couldn't we?"

Richard bridled. This was moving a bit too fast for him. He hadn't even mentioned it to his wife and he was pretty sure that she wouldn't approve.

"Susan won't be too pleased. I haven't really told her what I am thinking yet."

Roy didn't want this new idea to slip away from him.

"I will have a word with her," he answered. "In the morning."

He was as good as his promise and the next morning at 9 am, he was knocking on the front door of the large, stone house which opened directly on to Vale Street. In Richard's parents' day and prior, the door would have been answered by a maid, but not today. Florrie King, who lived in one of the workers' cottages further up the village and had had more than one assignation with Roy, pulled open the door.

"What the hell do you want?"

"I've come to see Richard and Susan."

"They are having their breakfast. It's early!"

"Dunt matter. They are expecting me." He pushed her aside and strode into the dining room, where he found the owners of the house eating bacon and eggs.

"I got this drawn up," he announced and threw sheets of paper on to the table in front of Richard.

"What is this?" asked Susan, picking up the documents.

"It's about the garage, Susan. Rich and I decided last night about me buying it.

She stared at him, "You've gone bust Roy, and you can't buy anything."

"Betty can though. If you sell it all to us, then you won't have the dirty old place around your neck."

Richard had said nothing, worried that Susan would go up in the air. Surely he had only agreed to consider renting to Roy? He couldn't remember anything about selling the place. Had he been that drunk?

Joan read through the documents quickly. "It says here that you are going to pay it all off weekly. And it's too cheap."

"Yes, but I deal mostly in cash and so I will be paying you extra each week - in cash. I can't write that in the contract 'cos of the taxman. Richard and I agreed last night."

"Did we?" Richard was not quite sure that he remembered all that Roy was saying. But he had been very drunk.

Susan Fawkes would never say to her rich but slow husband that she and Roy had a little history of their own. Not only was she the girl almost caught by her mother on the lane that day, she was also one of Roy's many conquests and Roy had never mentioned any of it to anyone. Roy was good at that, keeping secrets and calling them in later when it suited. He had collected a lot of secrets over the years. Roy winked at Susan and then drew his finger across his throat. Susan scowled and returned her gaze to the documentation.

"If you think that this is for the best Richard," she said. "And Roy must sign a separate and private contract about paying us cash."

"What about the taxman?" asked Richard.

"No taxman is gonna see this," answered Roy as he sat down and began to help himself to bacon and toast.

"Seems a good deal to me Richard, I want to have a bit of life while I still have some energy left," said Susan.

And so it was done. Roy bought the garage and surrounding yard and land. Richard and Susan spent more time away from the village than they had ever done and Betty Townsend looked after Roy as she had always done.

The Townsends had four children, one girl and then three boys all within five years. The eldest Barbara was a fat child and grew into a fat woman. Being fat does not matter in the least if you are happy with yourself, but Barbara hated every minute of it. Whenever she tried to diet, her feeder mother gave her more to eat and the more depressed the girl became the more she ate. Barbara was a miserable, fat woman with a fat and boring husband.

The three boys were trained by their father to ignore their school work and work for him whenever he told them to. Constant truants and full of their own self-importance, the boys were treated with deference by the townspeople. Any of them could fall into a fit of anger with only a little provocation and the remaining brothers would join in whatever trouble had erupted. The boys would fight amongst themselves, but never against their father. Roy had bullied them as he had bullied their mother, but he had hit his sons a damn sight more. Even in their twenties, Stephen, Gary and Andrew were afraid of their father and had the bruises to prove it.

The children coped in their own ways. Barbara married the uneducated bore from the next village and tried unsuccessfully to get pregnant. Stephen would drive the company lorries anywhere in the country, but would never leave the delivery yard at the other end. He had travelled thousands of miles and seen everywhere from the lorry cab and could not walk unaccompanied. He suffered serious panic attacks if he walked beyond the town and soon began to control his young girlfriend in a similar way. She was not allowed to go far without him and must return to him or home as soon as any errand was run.

Gary, the second son was a belligerent drunk who picked fights with smaller guys and had his band of hang-on weasels that would come in with another punch or kick as soon as Gary had finished his fun. He was a jolly, sociable smiler who won over those who did not know him and feared by most who did. He had been having sex with his girlfriend since she was 12 and she would do anything he said. He was not aware that Roy had had sex with her mother and that his girlfriend was also his sister. That was not until one of his victims told him about it during a beating. Gary had killed him and dumped him in the marshes where the body still lies. Gary kept his girlfriend in the dark and under his control.

The youngest Andrew was a conman. He started at school, taking dinner money initially and eventually progressed to dealing drugs. Few neither questioned him nor challenged him, fearing his brother Gary and his father Roy. Andrew cared nothing for people and that included his family members. He bothered not with the local girls and set his sights on the youngest daughter from the Manor. She, flattered by the attention smiled at him when she called for petrol at the garage with her mother and perhaps she took more care of her dressing when she was to see him. Her long, straight chestnut hair mesmerised him as she walked and her expensive but simple clothes silently swished. He did not think about what she and the family had in mind for her future. Andrew did not realise that was not of the right stock.

She told Andrew this one day when they were both 18, just before she left for Oxford and he was to work in the Garage office. So he raped her in three orifices and then came all over her hair. He made her swear that she would not tell her parents or he would ensure that everyone knew how much she had begged him to shag her. Selina stood up, wiped away her tears and tied back her damp hair into a thick ponytail before silently swishing home. Two village boys who had watched the scene in horror, stayed where they were until Andrew was well gone.

Betty Townsend guessed what her boys were like, but vowed to protect them from justice while she sank deeper into depression.

Roy Townsend didn't give a fuck.

Townsend Garage and Haulage grew from strength to strength and by 1985, they also owned the old Dairy which employed many of the townspeople and then immediately shut it down. They wanted to sell the land for housing. They owned several shops and one of the pubs and kept these open. Roy still had his sights set on the big farm on the edge of the village. The family there had belittled him and his family and considered them scum. Roy intended to own them too.

Farmer's son Robert Parry lived at Peatmoor, ten miles out of Tresaith with his fourth wife. He had married his first wife at 18 because he thought that meant he could have sex every day. He soon found out that he couldn't and so they divorced two years later when she caught one of her friends with his dick in her mouth. His second wife was a lawyer's daughter and very attractive. It took longer to persuade her parents to allow them to marry than he had expected. But eventually he did succeed and the two had a fabulously extravagant wedding, even better than his first and they moved into a lovely black and white cottage bought for them by his new in laws. This marriage lasted five years even though she knew Robert was being serially unfaithful. She hoped that he would only have his flings well away from home, but was brought to her senses when she came home early and saw him fucking her friend while she lay across the breakfast table. They divorced and Robert met his third wife, a young woman who worked in the office at the Townsend Garage in Tresaith. He moved into the cottage she had inherited from her Nain and took control of her life. They had a son, although Robert became convinced that he was not the father as he hadn't managed to sire a child previously. Gwen knew he was the father for sex with Robert was bad enough without her seeking sex elsewhere.

Gwen also had problems with Roy Townsend touching her up in the office and making subtle comments such as, "If you come here and sit on my knee, I will show you how to have a good time." Really, he said that. When she replied that she wasn't interested, he accused her of being a lesbian and said that a good shagging would soon sort out her miserable face.

Gwen had been present at the pub with Robert and the Townsends one Saturday night before she had her son and could avoid the experience. She listened to conversations such as,

"I wish I could go back home from here, turn on all the lights and shout, I'm home! Without her complaining and moaning that I am drunk again."

"And run into the bedroom banging the bed and ripping the blankets off."

"And saying, it's Saturday, behave like a proper wife!"

There was much jollity amongst the men and Gwen leant back and stared at the ceiling. Robert poked her and announced to the group, "Come on Gwen, let's get home and I'll dress your belly!" Gwen looked horrified and even the drunken men had the decency to appear abashed at this coarseness.

Gwen got up from her chair and stalked out of the pub. She drove straight home without waiting for him and when he was dropped off by someone later that night, she was rewarded with a good hiding and then he raped her. That was the night she became pregnant and she never allowed him to touch her again. Sexually that was, he would still knock her around quite regularly for refusing him sex. He seemed to think that it was the 1920's not the 1980's. She left him when the boy was two years old. He didn't seem to notice, having had several years of comfort from the fat girl who worked at the same office as him. Luckily, she was to inherit not only her Taid's farm but was also an only child and was to inherit her parents' farm when that time came.

When Gwen left, she took their son and lived in a small cottage in Tresaith which Roy had managed to secure for her. Robert had lost her house through his constant borrowing. She must now put up with a sharp increase in Roy's suggestions during office hours and sometimes his unwanted advances during the evening hours. Robert never, not once, came to visit his son nor take him out. Gwen fucking hated him and all his kind.

Lloyd Wright was brought up by a drunken father and a useless mother. He had an older brother and a younger sister. The children were united by a mutual hatred of their parents and the poor way they were treated. The family lived in a tied cottage on the Tresaith estate, where Dad worked as a cowman and Mum worked as a cook for Mrs Tresaith. The family were forced to church each week, until Lloyd and his siblings could argue homework, paid work or illness. His sister Pam became riddled with guilt if she avoided Church, sure that God was only interested in whether she went or not. She took to self-harming and pulling out her hair. His older brother Wayne began drinking and smoking weed from an early age and was known to the police for stealing a car and crashing it. Pam and Wayne died together in a car crash while speeding out of town one night.

Lloyd tried to avoid the stress of his life by being cool and popular. He was film star handsome with dark, thick, wavy hair and the girls loved him. He was not overly sexual, using charm and style to impress them. He wanted to leave Tresaith and study at University because he was more than clever enough. The Tresaith family recognised his potential and offered to help. Lloyd didn't tell anyone when he went to take his exam or attend his interview at Exeter College, Oxford. Selina Tresaith and her mother took him as Selina was to attend the same college the following year. They covered their tracks by telling his family that Lloyd was required to do some maintenance work at their Oxford flat. They arranged for a job for him in Oxford at a friend's restaurant and Lloyd was incredibly grateful. Selina and he got on well. They saw something in each other that was familiar, in spite of their obvious differences. There was no flirting, no electricity, just a comfortable friendship - from Lloyd's perspective at least. Selina Tresaith worshipped the very space Lloyd occupied, but had no intention of telling him.

When Selina attended college the following year, they often met up but always in a group. Lloyd had found his niche at Oxford and had friends who would not understand Selina. She maintained her gentile way of walking and talking and although not stuck up in any way, was most definitely neither a leftie nor a chatterer. She noticed that Lloyd had moved so far away from his family and Tresaith in his beliefs that he rarely returned home, staying at his job during breaks and starting a small business, organising locum staff. He hugged her with genuine affection when they met, which was often, but he did not contact her between those meetings. He didn't appear to have a steady girlfriend, but was never short of a date. Lloyd never asked Selina on a date and she minded about that more and more as the years past.

Dr. Lloyd Wright went to London where he was to further his studies into Psychiatry, his chosen speciality. Selina went back home to Wales and the two didn't meet for several years, although they often exchanged letters. Selina wrote an average 10 letters to his one, but that was better than nothing. She was just glad to hear from him on any level. Even when Lloyd told her that he had met 'the most gorgeous nurse in the world' and was thinking of asking her to marry him, she feigned pleasure. When he said he wanted her to come to the wedding in

Cirencester and that he was thinking of buying a house there now that he could afford it, she pretended that she was abroad that week and could not attend. However, Selina went to the church in disguise, watching from the street outside the beautiful church as the bride went inside a spinster and came out hanging tightly on to the arm of an exceedingly handsome Lloyd. They smiled and waved and Selina thought that Lloyd looked in her direction for longer than he would have looked at a nosy passer-by. Had he recognised her? She turned and walked further into town, looking tearfully into the windows of the shops.

Everywhere in Cirencester had such character and Selina thought about applying for the GP's position there she had seen advertised. This was the home town of the 'gorgeous' Mrs Deborah Wright and with luck Selina would be able to feign surprise when she came into contact with her.

Selina got the job for she was a consummate professional and her manners and breeding fit into Cotswold society perfectly. She bought the old school house in Upper Minety and lived there with her dogs and a cat and the ghosts which haunted it. She treated colds and ulcers and the menopause. She treated broken collar bones from hunting falls and pregnant women with their many issues. Selina feigned great surprise when she began treating Mrs Deborah Wright during her first pregnancy.

"You have high blood pressure, Mrs Wright. You must take it easy from now until the baby is born."

"But the baby will be ok?" Mrs Wright asked in fear. "My husband is desperate for a son and I have promised him one."

"I am sure that everything will be fine."

When Dr. Lloyd Wright discovered that his wife's doctor was Dr. Selina Tresaith, he knew it could only be her.

"Why didn't you tell me that you worked here?" He asked her, genuinely surprised.

"We haven't written since your wedding and I haven't been home much in the past years. I was very surprised when your wife came to see me. In fact I didn't know that she was your wife until she mentioned her psychiatrist husband."

"And will the baby be alright? And Debs?"

"You know I cannot discuss my patients with anyone Lloyd!" When she said his name, she felt her heart soar. Ridiculous.

"I know, I know." Lloyd patted her hand in an avuncular way and made her feel sick. He could still only see her as a sister, a friend. "I am glad it is you who is her doctor."

Poor Deborah endured a terrible pregnancy blighted by pain and depression. She endured two stays in hospital totalling four weeks. Her labour began early at the surgery when her blood pressure was too high. The baby was born dead in spite of Selina's assistance and Deborah died a week later in hospital.

John and Barbara Jones of Grange Farm at Pentre had only one child, a daughter Linda. Linda liked ponies and her father did everything he could to stop her pursuing her Pony Club ambitions. He liked his daughter as near to him as possible and it had been a sad day when Linda would refuse to sit on his knee and jiggle about. She no longer allowed him to stroke her to sleep and massage her body. She once told him that if he fucking touched her again, she would fucking kill him. She got a good hiding for that, with a belt and his stick. She had screamed for her mother for the first time in years, but the downtrodden excuse for a protector had left the house and was walking up the road to the shop.

There were many similar events over the years and even when Linda was 28, she still lived at home. There was no way she was going to allow her parents to handover the farm to her cousin who was willing to come and work there. No, she would keep out of their way and keep her horses safe and do the milking and work on the farm until something better turned up.

Linda's other cousin Darren Jones felt particularly close to her. He lived at The Mount in Pentre and spent all his spare time at Grange Farm. He worked for nothing, hoping that when he left school he would be offered a job. Linda said that she would speak to her father because they needed the help. She taught him to ride and helped him with his homework. She advised him on his love life or lack of it and taught him how to drive in the little Mazda she owned. Darren didn't fancy his cousin, instead he admired her and told her often that he would repay her as soon as she asked.

He listened with sympathy during the summer evenings when she complained about her parents. He had witnessed the way he treated Linda and was appalled by it. When he told his mother she said that John had always been a bully and a pig and that Barbara had been well aware of that when she married him.

"She wanted him because her family was skint and John Jones had money and had already inherited the farm and there was no one else to share it with," she continued.

"He is a lot older than her isn't he?"

"About 13 years, I think. He was supposed to marry some other woman, a farmer's daughter from Tresaith, but Barbara put a stop to that. "

"How?" asked Darren.

"The usual way, she got herself pregnant. Although we were all pretty well convinced that Linda isn't John's."

"So who do you think her father is?" asked Darren, riveted by this news.

"We all said it was that Roy Townsend. They were certainly a thing around that time."

"From the garage? He's a pig."

"He is a pig, always was. But I and quite a few others think that Linda is his daughter."

"Does she know?"

"I don't think so and I shouldn't tell her either. It'll cause all sorts of problems. She can't stand John anyway and if she finds out that he isn't her father…"

"She wouldn't inherit the farm?" Darren answered.

His mother was taken aback, she hadn't been thinking that at all.

"Well, it's probably best that you don't tell anyone," she said.

"Sounds like people know already."

"I am not so sure about that. That's the thing about gossip, the people being gossiped about don't always know that it is happening."

"That's a bit mean."

"Perhaps, but it has always been that way."

"Oh," Darren stopped the conversation there and thought for a long time.

In July later that year, Linda ran out of the house and told the neighbours that her father had shot her mother and was threatening to shoot her. When the police finally broke into the farmhouse, they found both parents' dead from gunshot wounds and Linda being supported and comforted by near neighbours. Eventually Linda inherited the farm and all the land that went with it.

In an apparently unconnected incident, Darren Jones was found three weeks later in the woods after shooting himself in the face.

Linda did not attend the funeral saying that she had been too badly affected by her parents' funeral to go to another so quickly.

CHAPTER TWO

Tresaith Asylum had been built in 1844 on land owned by the Tresaith family. Huw Tresaith had a troublesome, lunatic wife and he wanted rid of her. Although his doctor was quite happy to have her sent to an asylum, there were none in Wales and she would have to go to England. This was the lot of any mentally ill Welsh, they must travel to England and not understand the language spoken and not be understood.

Huw assembled a group of charitable investors and soon had all the finances required to build the asylum. Huw Tresaith ensured that he owned the building contracts and also the contract to supply meat, dairy and wheat produce to the Asylum from Fferm Eglwys, one of his own farms. Gwen Tresaith spent the rest of her days there but at least the children were able to visit, although they rarely did.

Apart from two or three breaks due to exam failure or sheer unwillingness, there was always a Tresaith in the position of Superintendent at the asylum. Even in 1985 the Tresaith family still had a good deal of influence over Tresaith Asylum via committees and councils and as businessmen. But there had not been a Tresaith in overall charge since 1968 when Dafydd Tresaith retired with ill health and there had been no one suitable to take over. The only Tresaiths around were Selina and her siblings and they were all too young. They brought in a Scotsman called Colin Watson who learnt Cymraeg in order to communicate with staff and patients and who was quite a success once he discovered how the asylum really worked. But he had left to tour Europe and then go home to Edinburgh to write his novel while he was still young enough so to do.

Dr. Selina Tresaith was to take over as Superintendent having completed her qualifications and her sojourn in Cirencester. She persuaded her old friend Dr. Lloyd Wright to take over as 'Head of Severe and Dangerous Disorders.'

Lloyd had travelled abroad for a while after the death of his wife and spent three years working in Canada. He had begun to feel homesick and so when the offer of the job at Tresaith Asylum came to him from the Health Board after a recommendation, he had been happy to accept. It had come as a surprise when he realised that Selina was the man in charge.

"Aren't you too young to be in charge?" he had asked on the first day at work.

"I don't know," she answered. "But I am in charge nonetheless."

"Yes, I am sorry, I didn't mean to be rude. I am a little out of practice in social niceties recently." He thought that he was probably still pissed off with the way Selina had looked after his wife. He had a suspicion that she had missed some early signs of toxaemia in Deborah. But, perhaps he was just looking for a scapegoat.

"Don't worry about that Lloyd, you will soon back in the swing of things here. I may be young, but I know everything about this place. I know all its history and funny ways and I understand the best way to make it work. I have been brought up with all the stories of this place."

"It's just an asylum, Selina. Mentally ill patients are the same the world over and we treat their illnesses the same way."

Selina looked at him over her glasses and half smiled.

"You have got a lot to learn Lloyd, wait and see."

Lloyd didn't have that long to wait before he discovered that Tresaith Asylum was crazier than he could ever have imagined.

It began on his fourth month there. Prior to that, there had been the usual rounds of assessments, Electric Shock Therapy and Ward visits. Lloyd found that he needed to keep his wits about him for many reasons. The staff, doctors, nurses and civilian staff all appeared to resent and distrust him. Lloyd assumed that they did not approve of such a young man taking over the senior position when more experienced doctors had been working at Tresaith for years.

Tresaith Asylum was a massive east facing gothic building with a myriad of wings which had been added on throughout the years. The early mid Victorian buildings were tall and architecturally adventurous and had echoes of Tresaith Manor. Later additions had followed a similar style as they progressed westward and then north and south from each wing. The first additions resembled a comb from the air, with the original building forming the comb spine. But then in the style of a doodle, extensions joined some of the comb's teeth and then extended westwards again. As the years passed and costs went up and income went down the extensions were less elaborate and shoddier. The comfortable wards which had once been near the front door and the offices were pushed further back. The views the patients once had were of the range of hills to the east and the rolling countryside surrounding the asylum. They could see the farm from where their food came and they waved at the workmen as they went about their business. From the front windows they could see their friends arrive by foot, horse and carriage as they travelled up the long drive leading from the Tresaith road outside.

Through the expansions, the patients gradually moved further and further back into the extensions, some on wards and some into tiny cells with heavy wooden doors and tiny metal grilles that had once been kept for the dangerously insane. All doors were locked once anyone left the original building. It had been easier over the years to move the inmates into the newer sections and allow staff and visitors to use the glorious wood panelled rooms with the excellent décor situated nearer the front.

The mortuary, a small building with an office, a post mortem room and body fridge sat opposite the church. This church, impressive enough when first built was sumptuously extended around 1888 in order to accommodate the large number of attendees. There was a machine shop, workshop and garages where machinery was fixed and maintenance men sorted out any problems with operating equipment and from where they fixed doors and locks. The kitchens were in one of the newer extensions to the south, but near enough to the staff dining rooms and main offices to ensure their food was delivered nice and hot. The patient's food tended to be simpler and colder, particularly as the large trolleys and cabinets took a damn sight longer to reach their wings and wards.

There were tennis courts and cricket pitches, a dance hall and a theatre. Lloyd learnt that for the past hundred years, all of these facilities were used mainly by staff and it was only rarely on Royal celebrations and Christmas time they were used by patients. But mainly, the clubs and church socials and the choir and the sports teams and the drama group and the painting class and the… were all attended by the staff. There were trips to the coast and to pantomimes. Trips to Liverpool shopping and visits from dignitaries. There were fetes and fairs held in the grounds as fundraisers for the patients, where only a select few were allowed to attend. They chose patients who looked the least scary and could wear the clothes of the day without pissing themselves or screaming for help. There had nevertheless, been a few events over the years where a patient had calmly asked a visitor to please help them, please take them away, please report what was really happening. But of course if a supposedly mad person tells you they are really sane – you know how that sounds. These patients didn't trouble anyone again, operations, invasive examinations and during the last ten years or so, heavy drugs saw to that.

That was an aspect of modern psychiatry of which Lloyd approved. Drugs meant that they could be more lax with the locked doors. All units were locked, but the patients could integrate with each other a little more. But they were all shadows of their former selves and shuffled about their common areas. Those considered a particular danger were still kept in cells and only allowed out in a strait jacket. More of the patients were able to socialise and that could only be a good thing. Lloyd did have a few ideas on experimentational treatments and hoped that he would be allowed a free hand in that regard.

Officially the building should have been referred to as the Clwydian Mental Hospital from 1983, but no one called it that unless writing on official documents.

Tresaith Asylum was overcrowded and there was no money for more beds and no wings had been constructed since the 40's. A couple of lift shafts had been built and these were decidedly utilitarian and for the benefit of the staff only. The patients were rarely allowed to use the lifts unless flat out on a trolley bed or in a mortuary box.

Nearly all of the corridors and stairwells were almost dark. There were lights, but to be honest they were rubbish. Some of the wings were linked by corridors half glassed and were great during the day although at night the reflected light from the wards across the small courtyards gave only a shimmery glow. When there were fewer staff on at night, the shadows were unnerving. And that was the problem Lloyd had. Although he knew all the patients were locked up, either in cell or wing, it still felt as though there were people scurrying round the shadows.

He was walking down one of these corridors one night when he met a woman he hadn't seen before. She wasn't any patient or a member of staff as far as he was aware. She stopped in front of him.

"Are you Superintendent Tresaith?" she asked. Lloyd noticed how well she spoke, with excellent diction.

"No, I am Dr. Wright. I am a psychiatrist here."

"A psychiatrist? Are you going to examine me? I haven't spoken to anyone in such a long time, the ward rounds seem to miss me," she announced sadly.

"I am sorry, what ward are you on? What is your name? I will make sure that you are seen tomorrow."

She smiled at him and said, "My name is Mrs Tresaith, Gwen Tresaith."

She smiled and walked on her way as Lloyd continued on his, while writing down her name on his notepad.

"Do we have a Gwen Tresaith in here?" he asked Selina, when he reached the front offices.

Selina looked up from her desk and at him with interest, "Aaaah, spotted her already?"

"She stopped me on the corridor leading to Chester wing just now. Is she staff? A relative? She seemed very nicely dressed for a patient and I haven't seen her name anywhere."

Selina smiled at him and said, "She is a relative, or was. Gwen has been dead over a hundred years, but she hasn't left yet apparently."

"You mean, like a ghost?"

"I suppose so. To me being a ghost infers something that tries to scare you by blurring around a room or going 'Oooooh' in your face. Nain Gwenny doesn't do that, she talks normally."

"She died a hundred years ago? Are you being serious? That's a fucking ghost!"

"You are funny Lloyd and as you haven't yet understood that you are on Tresaith territory now, I shall forgive you."

"I don't know what you are talking about Selina."

"Not everyone in the Asylum is like they are outside the boundaries. Your training has taught you that patients are mentally ill and must be cured. We consider them to be in a different mental state. That is all. We also believe that death is a state of mind too. Dead or alive, you can be where you want to be."

Lloyd looked at his friend and asked, "Selina, are you on some kind of medication?"

CHAPTER THREE

"Medication? No! I am a giver not a receiver!"

Lloyd wasn't too sure how to answer that. He also wasn't sure how to enquire further about the ghostly ancestor and so instead went over to the kettle to make coffee. He lifted the coffee jar and shook it at Selina, she nodded ascent in response. He made two cups and thought before he said, "What the hell do you mean about that woman? I mean- I don't understand."

"Drink your coffee, finish your reports and I will take you on an adventure. But what you see and what you hear, you must not speak of outside this place."

"I can't promise that. I don't know what I am going to see and if there is any form of abuse or poor medical conduct, I will not be able to keep quiet."

"There's nothing like that. There used to be before the 60's but not now. I used to hear some tales when I was a girl at home and sometimes brought here on visits and learnt a bit more. You know, we have records dating back to the beginning in our library at home? You could learn about it too. Do you want to read the records? I could get them for you."

Lloyd chose to ignore these ramblings, feeling that Selina must have taken something recently to make her talk like this.

"Sure, I would love to read the records sometime and yes, why not, let's go for a tour of the hospital."

He continued with the coffee and reached for a couple of biscuits which he proceeded to dip. Deborah hated it when he did that – used to hate it. He found that he corrected himself less and less in regard to his late wife. Perhaps he was beginning to stop missing her. He had loved her when they married - perhaps it was becoming more difficult to remember. Married life had been less than he imagined it was going to be, far less. There had been much less sex than he had expected and what there was, was clinical - lights off and nightie on. It was amazing that she got pregnant, but she did. Deborah's pregnancy had multiplied her anxieties by ten and there was now no touching and no tenderness. He had taken to shagging the nurse he worked with and had been in the middle of a quickie, when the phone rang and he got the news that Deborah and the baby were in trouble. The horrible thing was that his dick was stuck inside Julie because of the shocking announcement and they had to wait five minutes before it fell out. He and Julie didn't do it again after that. Lloyd had hardly done it at all since that night – he was too scared.

Since seeing Selina again, first at the interviews and now every day at work, he had noticed that she filled his mind rather a lot. When he saw her at Cirencester at his wedding, he almost screamed at her to come and save him, but instead he pretended he hadn't seen her. He had mentioned to Deborah when they were sending invites that he wanted some of his friends from Tresaith to come, but she said no. She demanded no. She had seen his town and didn't want to be reminded of Lloyd's roots and that bothered Lloyd. He liked his roots, was proud of them and didn't want to pretend that Tresaith wasn't his roots. Perhaps he didn't miss his wife so much after all. He was back in Tresaith wasn't he?

"Did you know that Deborah was so sick that day when she came to your surgery?"

Selina looked up and said, "Of course not. I didn't let her die Lloyd. Is that what you think? That I let your family die?"

He went red and answered, "No, I am sure that you did your best. It's still a bad memory," he admitted.

"But I doubt that you would be working here in this position at Tresaith Asylum had she lived, would you? She used to tell me that she had plans for you."

Lloyd stared at her, "You talked about me?"

"Only in the broadest and vaguest of terms. It's amazing what women can discuss, when one has her fingers up the other one's twat."

Lloyd laughed at this.

"She loved you and was looking forward to the baby. But, she wanted you to move to London and make it big there. She wanted you to make a lot of money and become some kind of famous psychiatrist by setting out an innovative treatment. She had your life planned out for you. Did you have much say in that plan?"

"Doesn't sound like it."

"No. Shall we go on this tour? Its 11 and everyone should be tucked up by now."

Lloyd drained his cup and stood up.

"Let's go."

Selina reached into her drawers and brought out a massive set of keys. They were each made from iron or brass and looked pretty old.

"Those keys look old," he said.

"They are old. These keys open doors that most people don't need to go through."

This tour was sounding interesting. Should he tell someone what was happening? But there was no one to tell, no one who would care except for Selina. That thought was an epiphany. He followed her into the wood panelled lounge area and they walked between the leather chairs and the oak tables.

"It's really nice in this building isn't it? I mean compared to the rest of the hospital? Even these offices are so old fashioned and so elegant."

"That's because the rooms haven't changed that much since they were built. Some of the places we use as offices now were consulting rooms and surgeries. Even though it seems a little close now that we have moved our inmates are corridors away. The staff and the mad used to live near to each other. They were locked in cells and rooms, but could often hear some of the procedures taking place. Some of the grimmer ones were done down below."

"In a cellar? Are we going down there?"

"We can if you like."

Selina went through a door off the lounge, which Lloyd had previously assumed was a store cupboard of some sort. There was shelving on either side of the door upon which was stored napkins, vases, glasses and other paraphernalia which could be used in the room they had just left. Selina didn't stop at the shelves, but went through door at the back.

"I thought that was more panelling," said Lloyd.

"There are a few places like this, in the oldest part of the building particularly. It was for the doctors and staff to conduct some procedures which they didn't want to make public. I think they also kept some particularly weird people down there."

"What kind of weird?"

"Extra weird," emphasised Selina.

"This sounds a bit like a Hammer Horror film. A bit predictable," said Lloyd.

"Difference is that you know Hammer films are pretend. Tresaith Asylum isn't. It's real."

He followed her into the darkness until she switched on a torch. Then he followed her into the torch lit room until she turned on the lights.

This room was laid out as a consulting room and although everything there appeared old and shabby, it had obviously been in use quite recently. Selina walked through the room, while Lloyd dawdled a little, picking up some of the equipment and looking at the diagrams on the blackboards around the room. The diagrams appeared to have been drawn recently and there was handwriting on there he recognised.

"Come on Lloyd."

He followed her out of the room and into the corridor.

"What's all this about?" he asked.

"Lloyd, just follow me and take note. You are going to see a lot of things which won't make sense. If I stop and explain everything as we go along, we'll still be here at

Christmas. Just look and listen and I will explain everything later."

Lloyd nodded ascent and walked along the corridor. He noticed that it was more dimly lit than upstairs and was going to ask why, when he remembered his agreement. At that moment he saw that the lighting was lamps and candles and these flickered as they walked past. He also noticed that the corridor was internal as the windows and doors which they passed, appeared to only lead into wards or rooms of some description. He wanted to stop and look and as if she heard him, Selina stopped in front of a pair of tall, oak doors. She took out her keys, unlocked the doors and beckoned him to follow her. This he did and listened as she said to the woman,

"We have a visitor, Mary. He is our new Medical Superintendent and I'm showing him around."

"From upstairs? Trustworthy is he?"

"Well if he isn't, he will soon find out the penalty, won't he?"

They both laughed and Lloyd smiled, not knowing whether he should. Mainly though, he was wondering why the woman was dressed in old fashioned clothes. She must be some kind of nurse. She sat behind a desk upon which lay a large ledger and in her hand she held bandages and cotton wool. This oak desk and she were situated in a small foyer office.

"Sally is being very restless tonight, Miss Tresaith. She has cut herself again."

"Trying to kill herself? I thought we sorted that out."

"The loop? It's always the loop. She tried again tonight – Christmas is coming and her memories have set off."

"If only we could break the loop for them. Shall I go and see her?"

"I will come with you and finish the bandaging. She should have calmed down now and she'll be pleased to see two young faces."

She pushed open the ward door and then locked it behind them. Inside were two rows of beds against the wall, fifteen on each side. The beds were so close to each other that Lloyd could not have walked between them. They must surely have to leave their beds by climbing to the foot and jumping off. They proceeded past the beds and through a door at the end, which the nurse unlocked. Lloyd noticed that heads were raised as they waited for the door to open. He sneaked a look and thought how small and thin they all were.

They went through the door, which was again locked. Lloyd had begun to recognise how far he was now from his car sitting in the car park outside the front of the hospital. His lovely red VW Sirocco of which many were jealous – he liked to think. He smiled and chuckled, which made his colleagues look at him, so he stopped.

When they entered Sally's room, Lloyd had expected a different sight, what that sight should be he didn't really know. What the sight was in fact – was a small woman with long, unruly hair who was strapped to the bed. Her arms and legs were bound by leather straps with large buckles. She wore thin cotton underwear, a camisole top and long knickers. Hanging over the cupboard door in the corner of the room was a long blue gown with lace trimmings. He was about to say that these clothes are Victorian surely? But he stopped himself.

The nurse and Selina cleaned Sally's wounds and applied antiseptic cream and bandages. Sally smiled at them and talked and muttered like an old lady while they attended to her.

"Now Sally, you mustn't do this again, you don't want to meet God earlier than he wants to see you do you? You stay here with us and we will look after you. We shall leave these straps on you over night, but if you promise to be good tomorrow, we will remove them."

Sally appeared to understand and closed her eyes. The threesome left the room and Selina beckoned to the nurse to open the grille cover on the next cell.

"Look in there, Dr Wright."

This he did and after looking, he stepped back in shock and then looked again.

"That man, he looks like…"

"That's because it is," answered Selina.

The man wore a black frock coat and trousers, a tall hat and spectacles. He was spectacularly moustachioed. He sat at a desk, writing with great focus. This was getting dafter by the minute.

The group retraced their steps to the nurse's office, which let them out into the corridor and locked the door behind them.

"Selina, what is going on here? I don't understand it."

"Lloyd, I said wait until the end of the tour!"

She led him further along the corridor and then they turned right down a connecting corridor and sometimes left. They must have passed a dozen ward doors, maybe more. Eventually they reached a doorway in front of which they stopped.

"This room is for the patients who don't need locking up quite so securely. They will mostly be in their beds, but some will be up."

Inside the room were four men playing snooker and drinking and smoking. They were dressed in Victorian clothing and when they spoke, Lloyd noticed that their speech seemed old fashioned and gentrified somehow. They did not present themselves as ill or mentally damaged in any way. Lloyd felt that he was in a heightened state of anxiety because he couldn't understand where he was and what he was experiencing.

Selina was talking to the men about their game and how they had enjoyed their supper.

"Is there any news from home, Dr Tresaith?" asked one.

"I believe that you are to expect visitors before Christmas. Your family and friends have been so busy with the shooting and the hunting that it has been impossible to come."

"Ah, yes. The game season can be the very devil." There followed further conversation in regard to grouse and pheasant and fox which kept them happily occupied.

"Are the ladies retired?" asked Selina.

"They went abed an hour ago."

"That is a shame. I wanted to introduce our Dr Wright to everyone."

"Bring him to tea tomorrow then! Or dinner! The ladies will let us know what is for the best."

"I shall do that. Goodnight gentlemen!"

Selina and Lloyd returned to the corridor and they walked back to the foyer and lounge area of the Asylum.

"What have I just seen Selina?"

Selina poured them each a whisky and beckoned him to sit down.

"This is an Asylum of two halves - the official half and unofficial half. The official half is upstairs and you know how that operates." She waved her hand around the air surrounding them. "And the unofficial half is downstairs."

"Selina, why are the people dressed in Victorian and Edwardian costume downstairs? Is it part of their treatment? And while we are on the subject, why was that nurse dressed all Charles Dickens?"

"This hospital has always been in my family as you know. The Tresaith family built it with good intentions, well mainly good intentions. There was a requirement from the County and who were alarmed that all patients were sent to England. It wasn't too bad for the wealthy, but for the ordinary, it was worse than hell. No Welsh spoken in England. Plus they could be sent to an asylum for very little. Pregnancy out of wedlock, anxiety, being sad..."

"I know all of this, but I do wonder how your family has so much control over this place. The authorities should have more."

"Because my family have always had power and influence and money. It won't be for much longer though, that's part of my story. So listen please!"

"Ok. I'm listening, but I do have to get some sleep tonight, I'm on again at 7 in the morning."

"And so, because of the aforementioned reasons, my forebears donated the land on a long lease, to be reviewed every fifty years and then took most of the building contracts. They still do. There is a Tresaith involved at many stages through business, although it is not always obvious. In the early years, the county paid certain amounts for the poor and the rich or moneyed paid their own fees. But there was a limit put on the number of patients of either type and if this was exceeded in any way, there were fines. So, they began to do the only sensible thing that businessmen would do and that was to take in patients on the QT. Only patients with money of course, it would be pointless taking in extra patients for nothing. Families were happy to pay if it meant that their person was kept out of the public eye and in a place where they would be safe. And so the builders put in extra corridors and rooms and cells and operating theatres over the years without ever knowing that they were doing anything out of the ordinary. It was just a building job 'Up the Asylum'. They didn't use the same men for each job, so there wasn't much talk and back in those days, they didn't question their betters even if they did think it was a bit suspicious. There were records kept back at the Hall and the fees were all paid in cash – always cash. The patients were looked after by 'trustee patients' recruited from the regular patients who no one would pay attention to if they ever talked. The Medical Superintendent always knew and some doctors along the way. It is still in operation to this day."

"I'm sorry, I don't get why a family with money would be sending their people here in this day and age. It's not so much of a stigma now."

"They send the kind of people who might go to jail or otherwise be found by people they don't want to find them. "

"I still don't get why some of them are dressed from the olden days."

"That has been an amazing discovery on our part and yet because the whole thing has been done illegally, we can't publish the results. None of the patients we have taken in under the radar have ever died. They live in the mental loop we all recognise in some of our patients and because they don't see death and no one talks about death and everything is always the same. Well - they don't die."

"So who pays? And how old are they? And what the fuck?"

"When the relative who had them committed was going to die, they set up separate trusts which pay for the keep. We have lawyers in the family too. And our oldest patient is 153 I think, but we have quite a few over 100. And the youngest is a 30 year old woman."

"This is nuts." Lloyd was pacing the room and slapping his head, behaviour which had he watched it in one of his patients would have caused him concern.

"Not really. You get used to it. You will certainly get used to the money. But, it seems we running up against a problem which you are going to have to help with."

"Help? I'm thinking of going straight to the BMA with this."

"Don't be an idiot Lloyd. I will tell them that you have always known and anyway you want to help those poor people don't you?"

"What's the new problem?"

"We have been given the nod that this hospital is to be phased out and our patients distributed into the Health Authority system and some will be sent back into the community all drug fuelled."

"And the Health Authority doesn't know about your extra patients?"

"No they don't and we don't want them to know. We have five years to fix it or sort it out and I have no fucking idea how we are going to do it without the other staff or anyone in authority finding out. So, go back to your lovely house in the town and when you come back tomorrow, I want you visit Tresaith Asylum Mark One with me again and this time I hope that you will have a different take on the challenge."

Lloyd did as he was bid. He walked out the front door and went towards his car. He got in, but did not drive away for nearly ten minutes while he waited for his heart to stop pounding. When he did drive home he did not sleep a wink.

CHAPTER FOUR

When Lloyd arrived at work the following morning, he was informed that Selina had gone out and was unlikely to be back until after lunch. Lloyd went straight on his rounds as soon as the Matron told him that there were several problems which needed to be sorted out immediately. He accompanied her into each locked ward and dealt with the patients there. Some were strapped to beds – for their own safety – and some so heavily drugged that they sat and stared at nothing. There was no one here who he could analyse or give therapy to on over half of the wards. These patients would never get out of the hospital system. The other patients were on low dose drugs and these people Lloyd enjoyed treating, endeavouring to discover what had caused their problems in the first place. Lloyd Wright was a Freudian and he kept detailed records of his cases for the book he intended to write one day.

The patients he talked to always looked pleased to see him. They were pleased because Lloyd listened to them and some were already feeling the benefit of his therapy, particularly the women. Matron had even deigned to say,

"You are making a difference here Dr. Wright. It's good to see."

"Well, thank you Matron. That's a good thing to hear."

"I mean it Dr. some of our patients get worse the longer they are in here. I started my nursing in Oswestry and then qualified in Psychiatric Nursing and eventually ended up here. I've seen quite a lot."

"You are doing a very good job of keeping all the wards in tiptop condition. How many patients are you responsible for in total?" Lloyd was trying to find a subtle way to ask if she was aware of the other inmates.

"There are just over 800 patients at the moment, but when I started here there were 1500. 1500 souls, can you imagine? But I am responsible for the 88 we have just seen and the other eight Matrons have the rest divided between them. But you know all this surely?"

"I do Matron. It's just that there are so many patients, that I have almost lost count. I don't see them all obviously. I suppose I had a sudden feeling that this is such a big job."

"Not too much for you?"

"No, no not at all, I enjoy working here. I sometimes worry that I don't see every patient that I should."

"I think that you are seeing all the patients that you are supposed to Doctor, don't you?"

Lloyd was finding no more information from Matron and so instead, he smiled and nodded. He certainly had enough patients under his responsibility and was glad of the other therapists who worked under his direction. But did Matron know about the others? He didn't know the answer to that one.

He walked back to the office area alone. He had treatments to supervise today, although not until this afternoon. He should be writing up reports and treatment plans now, but thought that he might have another look around downstairs. He went into the same cupboard as last night and before he could make it through to the back, he was called out by one of the medical secretaries.

"Anything I can help you with Dr?"

"No. I – I was looking for some – err – paper."

"Come with me Dr. I have all that you could need in my office."

Lloyd followed her and accepted the paper for which he had no use. This wasn't going to be as easy as he thought. By the time Selina turned up, he had finished his reports, arranged tomorrow's operations, done today's operations and approved the week's rota for the doctors under his wing. He had almost forgotten about the forgotten.

"Have you thought much about last night, Lloyd?" Was the first question she asked when she saw him.

"Yes I have, in between my jobs and things." He was apparently losing the ability to speak like an adult. An adult Chief Psychiatrist at that...

"Have you come up with any solutions yet?"

"No, for God's sake Selina. I am still at the stage of not believing what you told me and if I do believe you, then I should be going to the Health Authority."

"I can guarantee that it is all true, and if you go to the Health Authority, all those inmates will be spilt up and taken to mental hospitals all over the place. They will be miserable."

Lloyd couldn't accept that this was his fault. How was it his problem? But he had to accept that this was an extremely well paid and responsible position and one he was unlikely to obtain at his age anywhere else. A few more years and he would have paid for his Tresaith house outright and could look for another property abroad -Canada maybe.

He would be daft to ignore that fact. "Shall we go again? I want to look at the whole set up while I'm not in shock."

She smiled and nodded and jumped off his desk where she had been sitting listening to him.

"Come on, let's go," she said.

Lloyd followed her and then overtook her. He wanted to see this for himself. He was going to treat this visit like one of his rounds, so he grabbed his clipboard and pen as they passed his desk. By the time they reached the first ward door in the old part of the asylum, the nurse from the previous day had opened the door.

"Ah, I thought you would be back Dr. None of you can keep away once you see what is down here. And none of you ever go and tell anyone else, do you?"

"I haven't told anyone else, Nurse. But then I would never speak of what happens at any hospitals where I work. It's not ethical, I it?"

"I'm the Matron. No it's not ethical, but that's not the real reason is it? It's more curiosity and research and fascination - a little of all of those. Now, let us see everyone in this ward and speak to them properly shall we?"

He nodded vaguely and stopped at the foot of the first bed. Matron began,

"This young man is Darren Jones. He lived close by here and was witness to the horrific murder of his aunt and uncle. Then the perpetrator of that crime shot him, so that he wouldn't tell anyone about it. He was brought here after the funeral and we encouraged him out of himself."

"Are you telling me he was dead?"

Lloyd looked at the man lying on the bed in front of them. He was prostrate and unresponsive to their presence. His arms lay neatly over the sheet and his pale palms pointed to the ceiling. His head was heavily bandaged with only the smallest slits for eyes, nose and mouth. His mouth slit was occupied by a tube, which Lloyd presumed was helping him breathe.

"Was or is. What's the difference? Death isn't what you think it is Dr. Wright. All of us die all the time and don't even notice."

"What are you talking about Matron?"

"Not learnt that yet? You will soon, don't worry."

"I don't know what you mean."

"You will. Now - Darren Jones came here on the instructions and payments of his parents. They believe that his cousin killed her parents and then killed him. Mrs Jones had worked here at the asylum for several years and so she got a staff discount. The discounts are quite good here you know, if you ever need them."

"That's good to know. I doubt I shall need it – not in this way."

"That's what they all say. She shot him really well and he was dead, or was called dead by the doctor who attended the scene. Darren's mother got in touch with us and we brought him here."

"What about the funeral and the authorities? How did you get round that?"

"He was brought here, it was a closed coffin and as far as the authorities are concerned he is dead. That's the same as everyone here, they are considered dead by all except the family who sent them here. We look after them until they decide to move on to their next dream world."

"I have questions here. Firstly, that means that Darren's mother knew about this section of the hospital beforehand and secondly, dream world?"

"I could spend hours explaining the second answer to you, but you will understand it much better when you have worked with us all for a time. Yes, his mother did know about here, she had done some shifts before and many since."

Lloyd walked around the bed to get a better look at Darren. His dressings were clean, as was his bed. He breathed normally, but shallowly and lay in the manner of someone who has been unconscious for a long time.

"Is he permanently unconscious?" he asked.

"No. He was in the beginning, but now has periods of lucidity. He wakes up and asks about what has happened to him. We tell him that he is in hospital for a short stay after an operation on his nose. He thinks that he broke it coming off his bike. His mother confirms that when she visits and of course he believes her."

"Is he getting better?"

"His face will grow back, if that is what you mean. It will grow back because he believes that it is only his nose that is broken and so he won't project any other problem. We are keeping him quiet until the convalescence is finished. No mirrors allowed, no negative talk and no talk of physical limits or death, or life outside the asylum."

Lloyd listened to Darren's heart and lungs through his stethoscope and found the young man's condition much better than a gunshot to the face might suggest. His colour was good and a look at the wounds showed Lloyd, that although much of his skin, muscle and one of Darren's eyes were missing, the injury was clean and obviously healing. Matron took over and adjusted Darren's bandages and smoothed his bedclothes. Lloyd noticed that this was done with great kindness.

"You are expecting Darren to recover?"

"Darren is recovering very quickly from his broken nose and will soon be up and around. We are thinking of offering him work here as he is so young and strong. He will help the community move forward and help the properly sick people here." This speech was accompanied by a finger to her lips and then hand motions which informed Lloyd that she only wanted to hear positive speech. Lloyd acknowledged and agreed with her.

Matron took Lloyd from the side ward into the next. This locked cell held the man whom Lloyd had recognised the evening prior - Roy Townsend.

"I know him and his family," said Lloyd. "Will he know me?"

"May do, he has only been here six months. His wife is here too, but they don't socialise."

"What is the story here?"

"There is a lot of history with the Townsend family, I expect you know some of it. Dr Tresaith believes that the real reason the family sent them here was to get control of all the money and the businesses. The Townsend boys sent their mother first and then their father."

"Since I left Tresaith to study, I have only been back twice for my parents' funerals and haven't kept in touch with old neighbours. They have all left Tresaith now one way or another and so, although I know what they were all up to when I lived here, I know nothing since. I don't consider any of the Townsends to be particularly nice people though."

"That may be so, but we can't judge anyone once they are in our care, can we?"

Lloyd nodded his ascent and followed her into the cell after she unlocked the door. He noted that she did not lock it behind them and had brought in a syringe filled with - he knew not what.

"Hello Mr Townsend," she spoke loudly. "We have a visitor for you today. Our new Medical Superintendent, Dr. Wright."

"Hello Mr Townsend," Lloyd said. He wasn't going to mention his connection to the town. Perhaps the old man wouldn't remember him.

"Hello Dr. Wright. Come for business advice?"

"No Mr Townsend, although I expect some financial advice would help me out on the salary I get."

He was going to ask why he was dressed as he was, but decided against it until he knew more.

"I like your outfit," he said instead.

"Why thank you! I decided to dress a little better than when I worked at... when I was in the other business."

"Mr Townsend was a very successful businessman in his own right until he graciously accepted our offer to run the finances of the asylum. We would be lost without him."

"Is there anything I can help you with, Mr Townsend? I'm on my rounds at the moment."

"I feel fine Dr. Wright. Now that I have been taught to read and write properly, I go over the accounts again and again and that keeps me busy enough."

Matron ushered Lloyd out of the room and when they were safely back in the corridor on the other side of the now locked door, she said, "He believes different realities every day."

"Why does he dress like that?"

"He met some of our older residents and wanted to dress like them. He has no real concept of his past life now."

"And his wife? Betty wasn't it? She seemed like a nice lady, although a bit dim from what I remember."

"She's here too. I will take you to her next."

Matron strode ahead before turning in through another ward door. This door was not locked and when they entered the room Lloyd soon realised why when he saw the occupant.

"Morning Betty! How are you feeling today? I've brought a new doctor for you to have a talk to. He's Dr. Wright."

"Hello Betty! Do you mind if I ask a few questions?" He picked up her clipboard from the end of her bed. Betty Townsend was sitting in a large leather chair.

"Hello doctor. It is nice of you to come and see me. I'm pregnant you see and will be giving birth to four children any day now."

Lloyd placed his hand on her shoulder and she smiled encouragingly. He began to gently examine her and was soon aware that one of her arms finished below the elbow and one leg below the knee. Her other leg finished was in a plaster cast. She had scars, bad scars on her face and around her body. They appeared to have been made with a chopping blade. Matron whispered in his ear,

"Her husband did it to her with an axe. She doesn't really notice."

"You see doctor, it's a miracle that I'm pregnant when I have these deformities, isn't it? Some might think that I couldn't get a husband, but I've got four children, or going to have four children. Are they still in my tummy, nurse?"

"They are, Betty. They will arrive when they are good and ready – you know what babies are!"

They laughed at this joke and Dr Wright asked her a few questions and took her blood pressure and checked her charts. Flicking his eyes around the room, he noticed that the pictures on the walls were of Tresaith village in the 1930's. There was no mirror, nor surfaces where Betty could see her reflection. He asked on impulse,

"Bathrooms, Matron?"

"Down the hall, men and women are separate, of course. Some patients such as Betty here have room service," she answered and nodded in the direction of the chamber pot in the corner.

Lloyd looked again at the horror which was Betty and smiled at her. "I will call and see you again Betty," he told her.

"Thank you Doctor," she answered.

Lloyd was thoughtful as they walked out of the room, "The Townsend family must be paying a lot for this."

"They can afford it," Matron said curtly. "They've been robbing people for years and are still doing it now."

The next call was on a ward of 20 men. They were intermittently sitting on their beds or on chairs. Others were shuffling around and some stared into space.

"Now these patients are paying less than the private rooms. The existence of some patients is well known amongst their ancestors, but they hold positions that would not be helped by negative publicity such as these family members. The unknown patients' bills are being paid by solicitors from the family estates after their near relatives died. They are never checked on and are either forgotten by or not known about within their families."

"Where do they think the money is going to?"

"Charities or just out of the family. They mainly are told that there was no inheritance or something similar."

"What happens to them if the payments stop?"

"That question must be aimed at Dr. Tresaith. It's not my department."

Lloyd walked among the men. They did not pay much attention to him and seemed healthy enough. It was plainly obvious that they had mental and physical health problems, but they were happy and not in distress. The beds were old fashioned and simple and quite close together as he had seen previously. He again surmised that the men had to climb out of the bed by shuffling to the end and clambering out, it was the only real solution. The walls were bare, with the exception of a large wooden board upon which were notes advertising tea parties and theatre shows. Other notes gave lists of names, which Lloyd guessed were the names of those in the ward – perhaps good behaviour status. There were no mirrors and the lamps were old fashioned and dim. He realised that he hadn't seen a window since he has come to this part of the hospital.

Visits to other parts of the hospital showed him similar wards, some male and some female. Some patients were quite elderly and unfashionably dressed. Many put Lloyd in mind of Ebenezer Scrooge and his Christmas Carol associates. They weren't scary or different to his usual patients, except that he felt he was in a different country. This was a similar feeling to how he felt when abroad, where even though people spoke English, they appeared to be members of a different club.

Suddenly he felt a firm tap on his shoulder and as he swung round he saw a face he recognised, "Hello Mr Parry."

"Thought I fucking recognised you, young Lloyd. What are you doing here?"

"I am the Medical Superintendent. Why are you here? I haven't seen you since…"

"I let you go beating!"

"You wouldn't let me go shooting."

"Well if you were as good a shot as your father, we would all have been dead!"

Robert Parry looked much older than when Lloyd had last seen him. Then he had been pissed and chasing some young woman at a fete, he seemed to remember. He couldn't remember whether Parry was divorced or married, but Lloyd knew he had inherited a farm from his last wife. Robert hadn't answered why he was here, perhaps he was visiting one of the Townsends? Before he could establish anything, Matron caught up with him and said to Robert, "Robert! What are you doing out of your room? "

"Taking a walk Matron. Taking each day as it comes just as instructed!" Robert had adjusted his attitude to a falsely jolly demeanour while talking to Matron, Lloyd noticed.

"Well get yourself back into your ward, I thought the door was locked. It certainly should be locked."

She ushered the obedient Robert Parry back to his ward, gave some sharp commands to a nurse there and returned to Lloyd.

"They can be cheeky bastards," she said. "We have to keep our eye on them Dr. Wright. He's a woman beating drunk whose family decided to put him in here instead of allowing him to answer for killing his ex-wife."

"The one he inherited the farm from?"

"No, Gwen, the one with the boy. She was my sister, so it's a bit difficult to remain ambivalent to him. I know I should and I mainly do, but as I said it can sometimes be difficult." Her voice tailed off.

"I can imagine. How did she die?"

"She was beaten to death by an unknown assailant, the police said. The boy was unharmed, but may have seen the whole thing. Robert went for custody of him afterwards, but luckily there was enough doubt not to allow that to happen. The boy lives with me now. He's safe and pretty well grown up."

"Does he know that his father is here?"

"No, nor that his father likely killed his mother. The poor little sod is screwed up enough as it is without burdening him with that news."

Lloyd didn't really know how to answer this, so he didn't.

"We are at the laundry chutes now," announced Matron. "The laundry from down here is sent upstairs to join the main hospital laundry."

"I don't get how these patients are not known about in the local authorities."

"Some know, some don't. It's the same with everything isn't it?"

The laundry chutes were nothing more than huge round metal doors with hinges and turn locks. There were two, side by side. Lloyd opened one to reveal a metal duct with a metal sleeve containing a cradle. This was evidently where the laundry was sent to be dealt with and brought back.

"How do get to the mortuary from here?"

"Surely Dr. Tresaith told you? We don't need the mortuary. No one has ever died here. Ever."

CHAPTER FIVE

By the time Lloyd had worked at Tresaith Mental Hospital for a year, everything felt normal. The upstairs and the downstairs patients never met and he found it surprisingly easy to switch his modus operandi between the two. He was recognised and respected wherever he went throughout the hospital. He was settling into his house in the town and had already attracted attention amongst the local singletons. Once his widowhood had been sadly acknowledged and sincere condolences passed on, quietly probing questions began about potential girlfriends. Lloyd told them that he was still grieving for his lost family and ambitions and wanted to concentrate on his career for a while. They presented sad faces and undeterred, kept mental determinations to break down this unwelcome resolve.

Selina Tresaith thought differently. Lloyd was in her sights, she would use her power both monetary and career wise and she would see off any competition however it presented itself.

"I have had another letter this morning, Lloyd."

The two of them were in the main office off the reception area, discussing patients and staff. This meeting was weekly and separate to the weekly meetings they held with all staff seniors on these same subjects. Another weekly meeting involved the senior staff from the downstairs asylum. A further monthly meeting was with those of the Health Authority to discuss progress and problems. The meeting which we are currently discussing had more truth spoken than in all the others combined.

"They said the closure is definitely coming, any ideas yet?"

"No. I mean I've thought about it a lot. I've thought that we could perhaps bring the patients up one by one into the hospital and fiddle the books so to speak."

"That's getting harder to do, there are too many records being kept these days."

"Plus we couldn't bring up the ones who still have relatives who might discover what we've done. That's why we have to be careful."

"And there are still people about who will recognise them. It's only the really old patients they won't recognise and if they came upstairs they might die."

"I've been thinking about that as well."

"Bringing the old ones upstairs to die?"

"No. We would have to account for extra bodies and that would cause different problems. But there is another way."

"I almost dread you telling me what that might be."

"It's not a horrible thing, it's more like the end of an experiment. We treat the downstairs patients like we treat the upstairs patients. We begin to talk about death and illness and the real reasons they are here."

"So that they begin to realise that there should be an end to life. Once they start on that thought road, they will naturally die off."

"We will lose money, but we are going to lose a lot more if the authorities ever find out what we've been doing."

"How long have we got?" Lloyd couldn't say when he had begun to refer to this problem being ours as opposed to yours.

"They say the final date is 1995, but they will supervise the transfer of patients a couple of years prior to that. So we've got five years before they really start to stick their noses in. So far they have never done a proper thorough check of the hospital and knowing the way they always run it, I doubt they ever will."

"So you expect us both to be here right up to the closing date? I fancied doing a few more years abroad."

"Lloyd you have to stay and help. I can't do this on my own. As it is I'm going to have to pay off the downstairs staff, although I'm sure they will keep quiet. They are too well involved."

"I think we can let them go naturally now. You know, encourage voluntary redundancy."

"Manage with fewer staff?"

"Maybe. But the authorities aren't going to be sending us upstairs patients so much now and in a couple of years, they will start moving them to other hospitals."

"After all of the good work that has been done here, it's very sad."

"This is true. I would love to write up about how we have, well your family have, managed to keep everyone alive. That's over a hundred years' research, it's worth a fortune."

"It's not really though is it? No government wants to pay for a population that never dies."

"I suppose not. But I think that here at Tresaith Asylum, we are nearer to discovering something about the meaning of life."

"And death."

Lloyd took the offered cigarette and they smoked in silence. Their thoughts were interrupted by the head Medical Secretary rushing into the office.

"Both of you come quickly. We have a problem."

They hastily put out their cigarettes into the brass ashtray, an ashtray passed down the years and removed from the oak desk only to be emptied. Medical Secretary Alice was anxiously beckoning them to follow her. This they did and ran past offices until they reached the security door leading to the wards.

"Come on, you have to move quicker. You remember that shit? Well it's hit the fan now."

Alice unlocked the door and they went through. She did not lock it again and no one noticed or cared. There was an unusual energy in the corridor, one they vaguely recognised and did not like. One of the nurses came out of Clwyd Ward with blood on her face and cried, "Doctors, I don't know how to handle this."

They went into the ward at a swift walking pace, not wishing to alarm the patients there. They needn't have worried. Most of the patients were either standing tight against the far wall or cowering on the floor. In the middle of the ward stood one of the male downstairs patients, dressed in his Victorian nightshirt of calico and carrying a large carving knife. The knife dripped blood which appeared to be from the man - his shirt was covered in blood and Selina could see no other victim. She moved towards him and spoke kindly, but with authority, "Joseph, what has happened? You are bleeding, we need to treat that wound before it gets any worse. Just hand me the knife, will you?"

She held out her hand hopefully, but was unrewarded. Joseph kept a tight grip on the knife and looked at her, bewildered.

"Joseph, you know me. I'm Dr. Tresaith and over there is Dr. Wright. We have come to help you."

Joseph grunted and raised his hands, one still holding the bloody blade. His sleeves rose up his arms with the action and revealed several deep cuts across his wrists. Selina made a speedy diagnosis and saw that the wounds needed immediate treatment. She tried to reach the knife and Joseph brought it down smartly in her chest. The nurse screamed, the ward patients screamed and Lloyd brought a fire extinguisher down upon Joseph's head. Joseph fell unconscious and Lloyd issued sharp instructions to the nurses and secretary.

"Nurse Hickson, kindly move the patients back into their beds Nurse Rutherford, fetch one of the porters and move Joseph into a side ward. Alice, help me get Dr. Tresaith on to this stretcher."

They hurriedly wheeled Selina into a medical room and Lloyd assessed her.

"Shall I call the police?" asked Alice.

"No, no, we must sort this out for ourselves. If we involve the police – well, no one will be happy. Now, go and fetch my bag from my office and bring Sel – Dr. Tresaith's bag here too."

Medical Secretary Alice asked no further questions and ran to fetch the bags. She loved her job and the two superintendents, to be honest and would do nothing to cause them trouble. When she left, Lloyd spoke quickly to Selina,

"Selina, Selina! You must wake up, do it now. We have problems and I need you to wake up, because it's all happening and I am not doing it all on my own."

Selina stirred and moaned. She whispered, "I've just seen the light, the tunnel, whatever it is. It's real Lloyd, it's real."

"Well don't fucking go down it yet. I'm not handling this on my own."

Alice ran back into the room and threw the bags at him. He worked quickly, happy to discover that the knife had hit her collar bone and deflected enough to prevent serious damage. The bump on the back of her head appeared to have knocked her unconscious and added to her woes. Within half an hour, they had the wounds dressed and the colour flooding back to her cheeks. She half sat up and said, "I'm back. I didn't go to the light!"

"The light?" asked Alice.

"Don't ask," answered Lloyd.

They managed to clear up the mess in their immediate vicinity and the bloody mess around the ward. The nurses had calmed the patients and put them back into a routine. Lloyd steeled himself for the visit to Joseph and told Alice to stay with Selina, deciding that it may be best if he went in alone.

Joseph was sitting up on the bed, grinning from ear to ear and eating a bar of chocolate.

"We don't have sweets such as these in my ward, Doctor. Why is that?"

"Sweets are not good for you while you are supposed to be on a special diet. Sugar particularly is not good for you."

Joseph pouted and said, "I like sugar, I want sugar and I should get what I want. Where's mummy?"

Joseph was not going to tell him that mummy had been dead for over 80 years. Joseph had been one of the early intakes to the asylum in 1846. His mother sent him in as an 8 year old because they could not cope with him at home. He had hit the maids and taken off his clothes and paraded naked in front of dinner guests on two occasions. He refused to speak to his tutors and had a habit of hitting male guests in the genital area. He was diagnosed as being mentally subnormal with dangerous traits and was welcomed in as a special case because he was so young. It helped that his parents owned a good portion of property in Gwynedd and his father had friends in high – well, you know the drill. He was brought to the Asylum by his nanny, who did not descend from the coach. She handed him his bag and said that mummy would fetch him once he finished his schooling. Joseph sat on the front steps until one of the office staff came and found him. Joseph still believed that his mummy was fetching him as soon as he finished his schooling. No one had ever visited him and apart from asking at Christmas if his mummy was coming and being told that she was too busy, Joseph didn't seem to mind.

Lloyd had talked to him on several occasions and with the notes and consultations with Selina, Lloyd decided that it was highly likely that Joseph had been sexually abused by at least one of the servants. He had suspected his father in the beginning, it's often the father, but he eventually settled on a servant - possibly a footman. He didn't want to judge, he wasn't allowed, but he would dearly love to meet whoever had done the deed. What a tide of disaster he had begun. Joseph's mother had to produce another child to replace her locked away boy. Joseph had been the heir and when they explained to their contemporaries that he had died suddenly as a result of a fit, the couple had to work hard at creating a new heir. They had been warned that she should not have any more children, but Ffion Gruffydd knew her duty and had a further three daughters to add to their brood of five girls, until she finally produced the longed for boy. She was dead three weeks later, but the boy lived and took over the estate upon his father's death. He continued to pay the bills at Tresaith and his heirs did the same via a trust. Lloyd wondered idly how on earth Joseph could be explained in a modern world and also how they could ever settle things with the trust. Payments arrived every month and no one asked questions. It was the same for many of the downstairs patients. Those managing the trusts may never think of why they were making the payments. Who were the real crazy ones?

"Why did you attack Dr. Tresaith, Joseph?"

"Mr Townsend told me that my mother was never coming and that she was dead. I wanted to find out, so he helped me get up here through the laundry chute. He said I should ask the office right out. But I didn't know how to get there. So I was walking the corridors and then a nurse, who I didn't know, told me to get back into the ward. Then it was like my head was spinning and I could see daylight through the windows and everything was so bright and I didn't recognise anything. And I got very scared and picked up a knife and then everyone was screaming, so I screamed and then I saw Dr. Tresaith and knew that she had lied to me. Mr Townsend told me that you had all lied to me."

"And you stabbed her? That was not a nice thing to do."

Joseph suddenly looked sad and asked, "Is she dead? I didn't really want to hurt her, but has she lied to me? Is mother coming?"

"I don't know the answer to that Joseph, I am not in charge of your case. Dr. Tresaith is and she is also your friend who has your best interests at heart. Why has Mr Townsend been telling you tales which are upsetting you? Has he been doing it for a long time?"

"He always talks to me and he talks to others too. Mr Townsend has been telling everyone the truth."

"And what is the truth according to him?"

"That we are being kept in prison and not in hospital. People are getting a bit upset about it, I can tell you."

"Well, I can assure you that he is wrong. Tresaith is most definitely a hospital. You have just seen it for yourself, haven't you? You saw all the people in their wards and in their beds. You see nurses every day and you see us. You have always been looked after and never treated cruelly. Don't listen to Mr Townsend. He's a nasty old man who likes to tell lies."

Lloyd was going to have to do something about Townsend. He always had been a nasty old fart and hadn't changed during his incarceration. He took Joseph's arm and led him away. He beckoned the nurse to follow so that no suspicions would be raised with the other patients.

"Take him into my office, nurse. Wait with him there, I will be along in a minute."

Lloyd scurried along to see Selina and was satisfied to see her colour returning. Before she had begun to mouth the obvious question, he said, "He has been taken into my office. Once we are alone, I shall take him back and tell the others he has been transferred to another unit. It's Roy Townsend who has been causing the trouble. He's winding everyone up and telling them that they are in prison, not hospital. We are going to have to deal with him. How are you feeling?"

"I will live, thanks to you it seems."

"Thanks to your rock solid gentry' bones, Selina. You should rest for a while. I've stopped them from calling the police."

"I'm coming with you to see Joseph. And I think we should see Townsend too."

"I think you should rest, I want you well. Stay here and let me deal with it."

Selina was glad of this because sitting upright so quickly had made her head spin and want to throw up. She leant back and closed her eyes while Lloyd left the room and half ran to the downstairs wards. The nurse had taken Joseph into his room and already had him sitting on his chair.

"Dr., Joseph has asked that he doesn't see Townsend anymore. He is frightened that he had failed in his mission and that he will be punished."

"I agree with you Joseph. I am going to make sure that Mr Townsend is not allowed to talk to you or interfere with you in anyway."

Joseph smiled and sucked his thumb. The nurse pushed Lloyd away with a wave of her hand and helped Joseph into bed.

Lloyd was in a bad temper when he arrived at Townsend's door. He wanted to see the old man alone. He took the key to his door from his pocket and put it in the lock. He soon realised that the door was not locked and that fact annoyed him further. Townsend was supposed to be locked up and not allowed to leave the room unless accompanied by male nurses. Lloyd pushed his way in and saw Townsend sitting at his desk, dressed in his Charles Dickens rigmarole. He looked up as Lloyd walked in.

"Aha young Lloyd Wright, or as I should now refer to you, Dr. Wright. It's difficult when I knew you as the poor village boy with that tart of a mother. Heehee. She's one of the few women I didn't fuck – not that I can remember anyway. I may have fucked her and forgotten about it. Perhaps she was a bad fuck, or perhaps I couldn't bring myself to fuck her because she was scabby and smelly."

Lloyd took one step and hit Roy across the face as hard as he could. There were no witnesses and he enjoyed doing it to the old bastard.

"Get up Townsend and tell me why you have been trying to cause trouble amongst the other patients. You almost got someone killed."

"That's not the way a doctor should act. You should be making sure that I am well and looked after. I'm going to report you for that assault."

"There's is no one who will listen to you. No one cares about you. Your family are paying to keep you here and you will never return to the town or anywhere else for that matter. I'm going to see to that, you twat."

Roy's face tensed and Lloyd suddenly felt real evil coming from him, "You are a cunt. You always were a cunt and you have no hold over me. Don't cross me or you will live you regret it like many others before you."

"We'll see about that. I am the one with the power here. This is my kingdom and from now on you will have no freedom at all."

"And how do you plan to stop me?"

Lloyd didn't answer, turned round and left the room. He returned less than five minutes later with two large men who generally worked in downstairs maintenance. They grabbed Roy and began to strip him of his historical attire while he kicked and cursed and threatened. Lloyd ignored him and systemically removed the notebooks and pens from the desk into a case. He shouted a nurse and soon the group had cleared shelves, bookcase and wardrobe.

"This isn't right! You can't fucking do this!"

"You have been inciting these poor patients with ideas that are not good for their health. You've been encouraging poor Joseph to attack Dr. Tresaith. We can't allow that, it's a criminal offence."

"Get the rozzers in then and see what they have to say. They won't be arresting me when I tell them what's been going on."

"I don't think you want any police here Townsend. They would like to ask you a few questions about your wife and why you are hiding here. But, as I said, your family are paying us to keep you here and that's what we intend to do."

Roy Townsend almost went purple in his rage and lunged at Lloyd who ducked out of the way. The lunge was in vain however, as the security guards grabbed his arms and hurled him to the floor. A couple of kicks ensured he stayed there. Lloyd said nothing and the nurses following his lead, said nothing either. By the time they had finished, Townsend sat naked and shivering on the floor of his bare room. The only other occupant was a cot, bare of blankets.

"The family don't visit anyway sir. They won't know about what he's been up to," said a nurse.

"No. Hopefully he will stop upsetting the other patients with his scare stories. If they start to believe they aren't going home well…"

"Well indeed. Now let's get that stuff locked away."

They walked over to a door and the nurse opened it. Lloyd realised that he hadn't seen inside it before. There were shelves full of personal items along one side and furniture and clothing down the other. It was only as Lloyd looked properly that he realised how old fashioned everything in there was. He had become used to the patients downstairs and had stopped thinking of how old they all were.

"So much stuff isn't there? It's all been brought in by relatives over the years and never used. There has always been a fine line between making the patients feel comfortable and letting them realise that their life here is permanent. "

"Keeping everything the same is what has kept them alive."

"It is. And God help them and us if they ever find out the truth."

She shut and locked the door and left Lloyd alone in the corridor.

CHAPTER SIX

When Lloyd queued in the village shop for his cigarettes and paper, he mused on the fact that not one person there understood what really went on at the Asylum. Downstairs staff were always hired from out of the county - out of Wales generally. Upstairs staff, office and nursing, gardeners, carpenters, engine room men, laundry workers, tailors, upholsterers, water men, farming staff, kitchen workers, and woodsmen – the list went on, generally came from the local area. Almost none of these knew what went on downstairs and if they guessed, they said nothing. They were all well paid and anyone who had questioned methods over the years immediately lost their job. Lloyd knew that there was now a time arriving where communication was getting better and local residents were finding work out of town. There was also money to be made by selling stories to the media. Tresaith couldn't keep their secrets much longer unless they changed their tactics. It was becoming impossible to be able to hide their fee paying clients without someone saying something.

"Morning Dr. Wright! Busy day ahead up at the nuthouse?" Farmer Jack Jones was a bigoted old man with views more suited to a different time. People these days were too free thinking and liberal for a man like him.

"Good morning Jack. I have a busy day at the hospital, if that's what you meant."

"We all know what I meant. I'll be glad when they move all of those nutcases out of our town. My wife and daughters never sleep safe in their beds."

Lloyd paid for his goods, the queue having parted allowing him to reach the counter earlier. No one else said anything.

"They are not nutcases Jack. They are patients being treated for mild nervous problems. There are no murderers or criminals amongst them. Don't be so ridiculous."

If only they knew about downstairs. Lloyd left the shop, feeling irritated. How the hell were they going to get rid of the downstairs residents without heightening awareness? He walked around to his driver's door, but was shouted at from the garage opposite the shop.

"Lloyd!" It was Gary Townsend. What the fuck did he want?

"Hi Gary. How are you?"

"We got a note from my dad. He sounds like he is in trouble. What's happened?" Gary pushed his red pudgy face far too close to Lloyd's in what he supposed was a threatening manner.

"Nothing has happened. He has taken a tumble on one of his rounds of the hospital and is in bed. Why, what has he said?" And how they hell did he get a note out to you?

"He said he has been locked up and all his things taken away from him because you lot are trying to cover things up. He also said he is proper ill and needs better looking after."

"Well that is an untruth. But, as you well know he can only be treated within our walls so that the authorities don't find out where he is."

"I really don't give a flying fuck if the authorities find out where he is. It would save us a pile of money if we didn't have to pay for the old fuckers."

"And it will cost you a lot of money if the authorities find out they aren't dead and can answer for their crimes."

"And if these authorities discover what you lot at the asylum have been doing, then you lot will be in jail."

"So in fact it suits us all to keep our mouths shut and the money coming in doesn't it?"

Gary glared and then stood back. "I suppose so," he said.

Lloyd got into his car and lit a cigarette. The whole job was getting out of hand. Someone was going to find out and tell.

Later, when he could manage to get Selina on her own, he told her about Gary Townsend. "We have to move this plan forward Selina. The problem is beginning to take on a life of its own."

"I know. One of the downstairs nurses told me today that she wasn't happy without treatment plans and we ought to let the patients get some fresh air. Fresh air for fuck's sake!"

"I wish there was a way we could close it down quicker than we planned."

"And do what with the patients?"

"I don't know. I think that the more pressing problem will be to get rid of any downstairs staff who are likely to talk. Some are already it seems. Give them a good redundancy package and fuck them off out of Wales."

"And who would look after the patients?"

"I was thinking that we could get some of the more trusted patients to do the job. We can come up with a training scheme or something and tell them that they will be under our supervision and eventually there will only be downstairs patients and us."

"That's a good plan. But how are we going to get rid of the patients before we are closed down? And what are we going to tell the families."

"To keep getting the money you mean?"

"Exactly."

"I'll think of something. We will get rid of staff first and see where that leads us. Maybe before the end, we shall have to liquidate our assets and go abroad."

"Me and you?"

"You and me. That way we can keep an eye on each other." He ruffled her hair and left the room. Selina thought she was going to cry with pleasure.

"Alice!" she shouted. "I want all the staff details from downstairs. All the files."

"Should I ask why?"

"Money is tight. There may be redundancies, lots of redundancies."

"I see. What about me? Am I to be made redundant?"

"No, you are safe."

"Because I know so much?"

"Hmmmm. That and the fact that you are complicit in everything that has happened here."

"Well I know that when the end comes, you will set me up just like you always promised."

"Lloyd has come up with a plan. Slowly get rid of the downstairs staff and allow..."

"... allow the better patients to take over the asylum. Hasn't that been done somewhere else?"

"In a film I think. We will do a better job of it though."

"Are they likely to talk?"

"Who is going to believe them? Seriously? Anyone who talks knows the consequences, so they won't."

"I know."

"We have to start soon because we are running out of time."

"Two years, that's all we've got."

"We can do it. I know we can do it. Here are the files. We can start with old Mo Griffiths, she wants to retire to Rhyl."

"Wow, who wants to retire there?"

"Lots of people! Don't be such a snob!"

"Ok, type up a redundancy package. No wait, I don't want a paper trail, none of the staff should have any contracts or letters."

"They have all been searched when they left the building at any time. They can't have taken any files away. We have known them all for too long – it's safe."

"If any of them blab, I'll take care of them – of it."

Alice smiled and said, "I know you will."

CHAPTER SEVEN

Within six months the downstairs staff had been whittled down to two. Matron Hughes had been with the asylum for over forty years and was over 70 years old. She knew all the patients and they all knew her. The same applied to Huw Roberts, a man of all work and an ally of the male patients. Joseph was one of the twenty patients who had been given trustee status. Nursing and medical emergencies were to be taken on fully by the two Doctors and Matron Hughes. Alice also had her nursing certificate and could help if necessary. But, as they had not taken on any new clients since they had the news about the closure, everyone was in good health and apparently able to manage. Even Darren was beginning to look better – no oil painting, he never would be. But the gaps in his face had filled in and he didn't need so many dressings.

Roy Townsend had not been allowed out since the episode and was still not given any writing or drawing implements. He was apoplectic and was frequently heard smashing his cell door. Lloyd instructed that his food was to be given to him through the small sliding door and his waste was passed back through the same hole in a bucket. More often than not, Roy slopped his waste against the attendant in protest at his incarceration. All that achieved was a gradual hatred from the trustees and he received dirty food as they slopped his food back through the shit covered hatch. No one cleaned it. Lloyd told him to behave or life would become even more intolerable. He reminded Roy that there was no one he could complain to and that he would be better off being a good boy. Roy eventually appeared to acquiesce.

Betty Townsend was now well into her episode of senile decay. She knew she was married and had a family and still believed they were just about to visit, or had just visited. Time did not move on for her and any short conversations she had with the other residents confirmed her delusions. The Townsend family had been told not to visit and had taken little persuasion. They now had full control of all Townsend assets and Gary Townsend, after a lot of digging through the old storerooms at the garage, had stumbled across a fuck off big trunk full of jewellery, gold and silver. He knew not whether it was as a result of burglary or blackmail and cared less. At least it wasn't cash. Roy had been stealing for so long that cash could have gone out of date. There wouldn't be any problem selling this lot in London and no bank need be involved. There was a real temptation to stop paying his fees, but there was that threat of the police hanging over the family and so they carried on paying.

Lloyd was getting fed up of the whole process – this whole way of life. He had established that if people are not brought into contact with death, they do not die. This also worked in regard to illness, aging and the passing of time. People related to whatever was put in front of them. While the media like to tell everyone about their significant chances of getting a fatal disease and the need for organising their funerals at 50, they prepared to die. Here at Tresaith none of this was spoken of and the inmates reacted favourably to that. They lived each day in the same way, without feeling as though they were running towards an end goal. Lloyd had written much about the subject in his journals, which were locked away in his home safe. He knew that the only way he could publish his findings was to acknowledge the existence of downstairs Tresaith and that would result in a prison sentence. He had begun to consider the possibility of moving abroad, perhaps America and publish and lecture there. The Americans loved that sort of stuff.

Or he could infer that he had found the documents and there was a secret author. Or perhaps present it as a work of fiction and call it something like Tresaith Asylum. He would have to change the name though because he had no intention of being there at the end. When the authorities arrived, he decided that he was going to quietly and anonymously liquidate his assets.

Selina confidently walked along the corridors accompanied by four representatives from the Health Authority. They had arrived by appointment to discuss the allocation of the upstairs patients.

"I have grouped the patients who have similar conditions and have formed bonds which we believe are beneficial to their continued treatment," she said as made their swift way to the common room.

"That won't be necessary, Dr. Tresaith," answered Mr Jones.

"And why is that? We have spent a lot of time working it out."

"Because they will be moved alphabetically. It is by far the easiest way to move people around, we find."

"Does that not mean you have a lot of patients with similar names at each hospital?" she said with no attempt to hide sarcasm.

"We alternate the hospitals!" said Felicity Johnson, a recent conquest of Mr Jones.

"Will they at least be going to Welsh hospitals and within easy reach of their families?" asked Selina.

"When we looked through the records the last time we were here, there appeared to be little evidence of visitors," said Mr. Calcott, another non-medical young man with considerable authority – apparently.

"But the patients feel happiest when they can look out of the windows and see familiar sights and sounds. And the staff are all local and can keep them abreast of the local gossip. It all helps to achieve a positive outcome."

"We are finding that prescribing the more efficient drugs which are becoming available to us achieve far better and longer lasting results. We can turn them around quickly and have them back in the community quite swiftly."

"But they are on drugs and so not technically cured are they? They are only reliant on drugs." This was a pet subject of Selina's. In spite of all her secrets, which these idiots were never going to be allowed to discover, she actually wanted to help the patients who arrived at the door.

"Hello Dr. Tresaith!" shouted Lisa Griffiths, a patient from Ruthin. She was a doctor's daughter and after she had been left at the altar a few years prior had mentally begun to deteriorate. She had killed her pet dogs, butchered them and put them in the freezer. 'For Christmas', she told her mother. She would have been a candidate for downstairs, with her rich parents' fear of publicity, but of course, that was no longer possible.

"Hello Lisa. How are you today?"

"I'm fine thank you. Soon be Christmas won't it? Can I help with the cooking?"

"We will see. There is a lot to do between now and then."

"Indeed there is. You may not be here at this hospital at Christmas," said Felicity.

Lisa stopped combing her wiry white hair and said, "Am I going home then? No one has told me."

"No, no you are not going home just yet Lisa. We need a few more sessions with you before you can do that." Selina glared at Felicity, but refrained from hitting her smartly over the head with her clipboard.

Felicity was unfazed. "You will be in a different hospital by then."

Mr Jones looked apologetically at Selina and said, "We are bringing the date forward. We have to have the job completed before the end of March next year."

"It's out of our hands. Its financial and we can't argue with that!" Mr Calcott joined in.

The fourth member of the party, Mr Lewis, actually looked as though he was sorry and said, "I am really sorry Dr. Tresaith, we only heard yesterday."

Felicity looked up and down the corridor and announced, "and this decaying old pile will be closed down and probably demolished. These archaic Victorian buildings are nothing but cruel."

"And what makes you think it will be demolished?" asked Selina.

"Because that's what the Authority generally does. They will perhaps sell the land on for affordable housing, we could certainly do with some around here."

"I doubt that will be happening," answered Selina.

"Come along now Miss Johnson. There is no reason to upset the patients," interrupted Mr Calcott. He had noticed that a group of patients had heard the conversation and were now surrounding them and asking questions.

"But it will be happening, Dr. Tresaith." Felicity was not intending to give up.

"Tresaith Asylum is owned by my family, by me and has only been rented out to the Health Authority. We never sold it and so I can confirm quite categorically that it will not be demolished."

This statement quietened Felicity and her colleagues, but not the patients.

"You tell them Dr! You tell them where to shove it! We are staying here forever!"

"No you're not. The patients will have to move out anyway, this hospital is not going to continue."

This announcement changed the atmosphere in the day room. Patients began to move towards the group, eyes fixed and determined. They kept their arms by their sides and seemed to glide. The temperature dropped by almost ten degrees and the Health Authoritarians scurried towards the door.

Selina said, "I am sorry guys, I will show these people out and pop back in to see you. It will all work out."

As they made their way back to the office she said, "That was very unprofessional of you Miss Johnson. Rest assured that I shall be putting in a report about your behaviour today."

"I must apologise Dr.," said Mr Jones. "I suggest that you apologise too, Miss Johnson."

"No," she answered. "I have only told the truth." Felicity didn't like this stuck up doctor. Finding out that she still owned this vast building wasn't helping her mood.

They left and met Lloyd parking his car out front. Felicity Johnson gave the handsome doctor her best smile and hair flick. He didn't appear to be that interested as he nodded and went to the front door. By the time he went into Selina's office to see how she had faired, he was worried about the news she gave him.

"Fuck. That's a blow. What are we going to do?"

"Not sure what's next. Already I have fallen out with those four idiots you met in the car park."

"Do they have any power?"

"You worried they will find downstairs?"

"No, because unless one of us tells them they won't find out about it. I'm saying let's not antagonise them anymore so they will leave us to supervise the transfers."

"They want to transfer them all over the country. I mean England as well as Wales."

"Not Scotland or Ireland?"

She smiled at this correctness, "Who knows? Who fucking knows…?"

"We are going to have to make a choice you know."

"What?"

"Not get in the way of any of the transfers from upstairs so that no one ever wants to get in the way of downstairs."

"And after that?"

"I have no idea. We can't carry on as we have been doing. The whole support system is closing down. There will be no food, no staff, nothing."

"Well you will have to come up with something Lloyd."

"I will not Selina. I didn't start this, your family did - you did. They can come up with some wheeze."

"You helped it continue."

"I want out Selina. I want out. I want the money I am owed and then I am leaving. I'm not going to stay and I want you to promise you will keep my name out of anything."

"If I get caught?"

Lloyd shrugged his shoulders.

"I won't get caught and I don't want you to go. In fact I am prepared to say I won't let you go."

PART TWO

CHAPTER EIGHT

"We get calls night and day from the old caretaker now," said the desk sergeant.

"What has that got to do with me?" asked DI Revie.

"It should be to do with somebody. Ever since that asylum closed at Tresaith there have been trespassers there all the time. Mostly at night, he says,"

"Still not getting it," said Revie. "My days of dealing with trespass are gone."

"It seems that most of the trespassers aren't alive."

"Murder then?"

"No. More like ghosts. When Selwyn goes to check the place out, he says that half the time there's no one there."

"I've seen that place from the road. It's fucking massive so it wouldn't be that difficult to hide from an old dodderer who's pretending to be a caretaker."

"He's a decent bloke, boss. He used to work in the engine rooms there when it ran as a hospital. I gather that the owner lets him keep some sheep or ponies there in return for keeping an eye on the place. He's got a cottage there – it used to be the south gatehouse."

"You seem to know a lot about the hospital Huw."

"My Mam and Dad worked there and Nain and Taid."

"Seems everyone round here worked there at some point," said Revie.

"They did or else had someone in the family who did. There was the farm and the dairy and the gardeners and the…"

"Alright, I get the message. You all feel a personal connection to the place and don't like trespassers."

"It's not just that boss, they are starting to trash the place a bit and you know what happens to old buildings once that starts."

"Yes I do. The next lot wreck it a bit more and so it goes on. The Tresaith family still own it I think? They own most of the property around Tresaith, I know that."

"I think that's why it's called Tresaith boss."

Revie looked at him and nodded, he wasn't one for jokes. "I will go up there and have a look. Get the owner or the old caretaker to show me the place. I will be there at 3 today."

"Thanks boss."

True to his word, DI Revie was driving through Tresaith town at 2.55 pm. Tresaith was one of those Welsh market towns, which although had added housing estates over the years, remained essentially as it had done for the past few hundred years. Tresaith Castle, or at least the remains of it, stood at the pinnacle of the steep hill from where the town had grown. The northern end of the town lay at the foot of this hill where the cottage hospital and high school were based. On either side of Stryd Fawr and Vale Street were the large 3 and 4 storey houses used by the great and the good of past and present. During the past few years, some of these houses were being converted into solicitors or dentists and sometimes flats. There were shops and banks around the market area and John Revie noticed with pleasure that they all appeared to be doing a good trade. He hoped that the threatened supermarket would not be given the go ahead for the eastern end of the town. He turned left and began a descent which brought into view first the nurses' home which had serviced the Mental Hospital when it was open and then the hospital itself. It was easy to see why this magnificent Gothic building would be attractive to the curious as well as the criminal.

The main gates were locked and John got out of his car and pressed the buzzer. At the same time a small Daihatsu pulled in behind him.

"Hello!" said the old man driving it. "I am Selwyn Roberts, the caretaker here. I was asked to come and show you round and answer any questions you have. If you could just move along a little sir, I can unlock the gate."

"Of course, yes thank you. Are you the only one with the keys?"

"No, of course not. Sorry what is your name?"

"It's DI Revie. I've come about the break ins."

"Ah, the police are taking it seriously at last. The Tresaith family have keys and the gardeners and the different maintenance men. Mind you most of them don't come anymore and didn't hand their keys back in."

"And presumably anyone could have had copies made. Do any of these people have keys to the buildings?"

"I expect some people did, but if you think that these hooligans who trespass here use the front door, you are mistaken. "

"They break in?"

"Wait until I show you. It's a fucking disgrace."

He opened the gates and DI Revie drove through and parked in front of the building. It was even more beguiling close to. He got out of his car and looked up at the three storeys and clock tower with gabled roof.

"Like something out of a film, isn't it?" said Selwyn.

"It is. A horror film."

"Everyone who worked here loved the place. It was a proper village with every skill used here. I could write the longest list of the different kind of trades people used here. There was hardly anything brought in from outside you know, just coal and stuff like that. We had dances and theatre groups and sports teams and there were so many marriages after romantic meetings here."

"You miss all that now it's closed down?"

"I do, we all do."

"When was it closed?"

"June 17th 1995 the last patient was taken away in an ambulance to Liverpool I think. Lisa something or other - shame she was local and her parents ended up moving to be nearer to her. Anyway, all the staff left by the end of that June and the place was shut up."

"Over 10 years then."

"Doesn't seem that long ago."

Selwyn turned the large key in the lock of the front door and Revie followed him in.

Revie wanted to say that the place looked as though the staff had just walked out of the room, but decided that sounded too much like a cliché and so refrained.

"It's like they've just gone out, isn't it?" said Selwyn. "Could do with cleaning though. See those cabinets? They've still got loads of paperwork in them. I don't think they have the actual patients' notes in them, but loads of other documents."

"It feels quite creepy in here."

"Everyone thinks that when they come in here. But you are right. It used to be creepy enough on nights when all the patients were asleep, but it's a bloody sight more now."

"Why do you think that people like to come in here?"

"They think they see ghosts or demons or something. Some people just like the feeling of being in a dark empty place."

"More likely coming here for sex and drugs and burglary," answered Revie.

"That's because you are a copper," said Selwyn. "You think everyone is bad. Most of them are just idiots or nosy locals."

"So, what is it you want me to do here?"

"I want you to have a proper look round. The local guy came with a mate to check round a few times after I called, but never found anything. I've chased some trespassers away and spoken to the parents of the ones I recognise. But during the past few months, there have been lights on at night and some stuff has started to get damaged or go missing."

"And that's unusual?"

"Well yes. The electricity isn't connected."

"Oh, well that is unusual. Why don't the owners take the stuff out or sell the valuable things?"

"They probably wonder why, in this day and age they should have to do that."

"I suppose because it's always been this way. What I can do is get our Crime Prevention guy to come round and advise them on security. It will cost a bit, but worth it. You know businesses are getting cameras fitted these days. That certainly helps us catch the criminals."

"Well, I suggest you have a word with the boss then. They only let me have the land rent free in return for the bit of caretaking I do. But I don't want to get my face smashed in for that amount of reward."

"Have you been threatened by anyone?"

"I'm threatened all the time. It used to be that they just called me names and then last week I found that my horses had stopped drinking their water. When I went to check it I saw that the cables from the fencer battery had been put in the water so they were intending to poison or electrocute them."

"Any ideas who has done that?"

"No, but if I catch them, I'll fucking…"

"You'll call the police. Now, let's have the guided tour."

DI Revie found that he was as interested to have a tour of this hospital as he could be if he was paying to do it.

"Righto. Here is a torch, you will need it down some of the corridors. You want to see everywhere?"

"Why not? I've got a couple of hours and I'm not likely to come this way again, so let's do it."

Torches in their hands, they set off.

"These offices were where the admin staff worked. That was Dr. Tresaith's office and that's where Dr. Wright worked. They were in charge of the hospital when it closed down."

They looked at the wood panelled walls and the oak furniture and leather chairs and Revie said, "Where are they both now?"

"Selina Tresaith lives up at the Manor apparently although I never see her and Dr. Wright went abroad I believe. He used to have one of those big houses on Stryd Fawr. It's a solicitor's office now. We always thought those two would get together, but seems it wasn't to be. I think he went to New York or maybe Canada. Abroad anyway."

"Hmmm." Revie walked around the offices, trying the doors and opening cupboards. "This door is locked, got a key?"

"I haven't. It's always been locked."

They left the office and walked down the corridor and through heavy swing doors.

"We used to have all these doors locked so the patients couldn't escape. Not that they ever wanted to. It was nice here and they were all looked after like family. Staff and patients were family and it was very sad when everyone left."

"I bet. Modernisation isn't the answer to everything I find," answered Revie.

"You got that right," answered Selwyn. "This is one of the wards."

They went into the room, where there were six beds down either side. Each bed was surrounded by a curtain, all of which were drawn shut. Revie walked over to the first bed and put his hand on the curtain. He realised that he was hesitating slightly and so he swiftly pulled the curtain open. A shower of dust fell on him and he dusted his shoulders as he stared at the bed and a bedside cabinet which had a vase and water jug sitting on top of it. The bed was made up with sheets and a green counterpane.

"Are they all like this?" he asked.

"They are mainly. Each bed made up as they were when the patients left. The staff were very particular about doing their jobs and maybe they had an idea that the whole decision would be reversed. Nonsense of course. Then before they all left, the bosses told staff to leave everything as it was."

"Did all the staff leave at the same time?"

"No. They made staff leave gradually as the patients moved on. It happened earlier than anyone expected but still took a year to move everyone."

"It seems a bit odd to leave the place looking like this."

"Well the Tresaiths own the place, so I suppose it's up to them what they do with it."

Revie accepted the chastisement and peeped behind a couple more bed curtains and found the same sight. He noticed only one or two broken windows and he also noticed the spiders and the dust and the ivy trying to encroach through the windows. Nature was taking the place for itself. The surgeries and the operating theatres were still remarkably clean and almost seemed ready for use. For a second he thought he saw someone leave the theatre as they entered it.

"Is there anyone else here today?" he asked Selwyn.

"No, just us two. Why do you ask?"

"I thought I saw someone."

"Started already has it?"

"What?"

"Seeing ghosts. We all see ghosts here. Or don't you believe in ghosts?"

"I do believe actually. But it didn't look like a ghost, it looked like a person."

During their walk, they visited the kitchens, the dining halls dispensary and most of the wards. They went through the bathrooms, the attics and most of the rooms in the buildings. The hospital was in a pretty good state of repair and apart from the dirt, would have been able to accept patients within a couple of days. What Revie did notice, but Selwyn appeared not to, was footsteps, bangs, unusual creaks and faint voices. He was going to ask about them, but realised that Selwyn was either ignoring the noises or really couldn't hear them. Both scenarios were odd.

"Would you like to see outside? The mortuary and the church? There are also the workshops and the engine rooms. That's where I used to work. What about the nurses' home? There's a lot of trespassing there."

"Might as well while I'm here."

They walked out of one of the back doors and across a huge courtyard. Revie looked at the towering stone wings and annexes. Again he swore that there were faces at some windows and faint lights at others.

The laundry rooms were full of machines and dryers.

"The washing was weighed on those scales before they were put into the machines," said Selwyn.

The engine rooms were still intact and piles of coke heaped next to the silos. "The coal lorries brought slabs of coke from Deeside as well as coal. The slabs were broken with hammers and then the clinker from the boilers was sent back in lorries to make breeze blocks," he informed Revie.

"We boiled all the water here for the hospital and the nurses' home. Steam went out in pipes underground and cool water came back. We had to keep the boilers running all the time and that way the water coming back was still warm and didn't take so long to heat up again. We used to call it liquid gold. Ha-ha."

"Sounds like you enjoyed your job here."

"I did, Mr Revie. Find anyone who used to work at Tresaith Asylum and they will tell you a long tale about their time here. People used to go on a waiting list for jobs and often they had to wait for someone to die to get them to leave. We were all devastated when it closed."

"You are still here."

"I am and to be honest I would look after this place if they took the grazing away. But they won't, they are gentry and have always looked after the town and the estate."

"I look forward to meeting them all," answered Revie truthfully.

"Here we are. The church was built a couple of years after the asylum was finished. It's quite lovely isn't it?"

DI Revie walked inside the church and felt enveloped with warmth, before he quickly realised he wouldn't normally feel like that in an apparently disused building. This church did not feel disused, it felt as though the vicar had just walked out and the congregation were about to walk in - perhaps on Christmas Eve.

"We ought to get along to the mortuary now Mr Revie, it's nearly 5 o'clock and it's getting dark. I'd like to have the place locked up before it's properly dark."

"No problem, I can see the mortuary from here." They looked across the road to the door of the single storey building which sat alongside the isolation ward. The whole site had a great logic to it, Revie thought. Revie approved of logic.

They walked inside the building and turned left. There stood the room with the mortuary table on view and glass fronted cupboards full of medical instruments. Revie idly opened the tall metal door which he rightly assumed was the body fridge. It was similar to the ones at the county morgue, four racks high. Another reason it was very similar, was the fact there was a body lying on each rack.

CHAPTER NINE

Di Revie accompanied by DS Gwen Hughes, knocked at the front door of Tresaith Manor. The door was answered swiftly by a woman he soon discovered was a housekeeper.

"They are expecting you sir. Please follow me."

She led the way into a large room where two men and a woman were seated. The men rose as the police entered.

"Thank you for coming officers. How may we help you?"

"Anything you can tell us about these bodies would be a help," DI Revie said simply.

"We haven't heard much ourselves I'm afraid. I know you have found some bodies, Selwyn rang us and then we were advised to stay away by our solicitor."

"You rang your solicitor Mr...?"

"Tresaith. Philip Tresaith. This is my younger brother John and this is my wife, Sarah. Of course I rang our solicitor, he is on his way over."

"I can tell you that I was at the hospital after I had heard of the trespassing trouble you have been having and as part of that visit, I discovered four bodies as yet to be identified."

"How long have the bodies been there?" asked Sarah Tresaith.

"No idea at all, I'm afraid Mrs Tresaith. We will know a lot more after the post mortem. Now, when was the last time any of you visited the hospital?"

"Not recently, but I must tell you that our solicitor has asked that we answer no questions until he arrives," said John Tresaith.

"Oh! I was only intending to ask a few background questions, to help us with the whole picture. I am not accusing anyone," said the DI.

"I understand that and I hope you won't take offence, but we must do as we have been advised," answered Philip Tresaith.

"You are both welcome to some coffee if you wish to wait until our solicitor arrives," asked Sarah helpfully.

"No, thank you we have a lot to do tonight. Perhaps you will all be good enough to make yourselves available for interview, with your solicitor, when I can get round to seeing you?"

"Of course Detective Inspector. I will have our solicitor contact the station with his details and you can arrange it between you." Philip Tresaith considered himself to be exceptionally helpful.

The police turned around and walked out of the room into the hallway. A young girl walked towards them holding out her hand. DI Revie shook it and said, "We are police."

"I know who you are," she answered. "I am Carys Tresaith. "I hear you have found some bodies at the Asylum? I know a lot about how that could have happened."

"Carys! I told you to stay upstairs! Mr Revie, I have just told you that no one is going to speak to you and Carys is more than under age for your interrogations. Would you like me to report this to your superiors?"

"Don't be ridiculous Aunt Sarah. The police asked me nothing. I was the one who did the talking. And why should I not be polite and helpful? We all know things which would help them with their enquiries."

"Shut up Carys. You are too young to understand what is happening."

"But apparently not too young to cope with full time boarding school. Adults are so inconsistent." Turning to the police she said, "It was nice to meet you both and I assure you that if I was allowed to, I would help you with your enquiries." She smiled prettily and hands clasped behind her back, walked into the room the police had just left. Sarah Tresaith walked them to the door.

"Lively young lady," said DS Hughes. "Is she the daughter of John?"

"No she isn't and I don't need to tell you anything else. Goodbye."

"We learnt quite a bit there," said Hughes.

"We did and we should learn a lot more when we question some of the locals."

*

The overhead lights, police, fire and ambulance sirens and lights were causing great interest in Tresaith. As darkness fell, the drama commenced and door after door opened on Stryd Fawr and Vale Street to watch the vehicles speed past. Neighbours and ex-employees jumped into cars and were soon at the scene. Some jumped the fence and ran across the fields surrounding the building. They had been visiting, working and trespassing on the place for years and knew their way around better than the emergency services did. There they viewed the scene, noting all details so that it could be reported to their friends and family later.

By the time Revie and Hughes drove back into the hospital grounds there was quite a crowd in the fields and some people had managed to make it onto the driveways and lanes which wound through the site.

"Get rid of them," Revie shouted out of his window to a uniform.

"Yes sir. We are a bit short on staff at the moment, but we've got reinforcements arriving. They've called the specials out for that job."

"Good. As soon as they arrive, get them on traffic and security duty."

"Boss." was the affirmative answer.

They drove round to the mortuary via the side road, Revie noticing how dark the hospital looked now in contrast to the bright arc lights which had been brought into use.

"What was that?" asked Gwen.

"What?"

"Hmmm. I thought I saw lights at the windows of the asylum."

"You are getting as bad as the locals, unless one of our lads is in there."

"Maybe. But I do know people who worked here and there were always lights and noises coming from the place."

"You must know some of the trespassers then. It's difficult to see what's going on here unless you are on the property."

"Trying to get me to squeal are you sir? It's just hearsay."

DI Revie was not going to mention that he had seen the lights too. That wouldn't do.

"Hi John," shouted Jack Gainsborough, the pathologist. "This is an interesting one."

"Thought you'd like it, Jack. Better than accidents and murders."

"Very good, yes. Now look at these bodies, they are all prepared for burial. It has been done professionally and with care. It reminds me of how bodies were treated back here in the day."

"When it was a hospital, you mean?"

"I do mean just that. Same cloth, same laying out, same everything. I will know more when they are back at base, but at the moment they seem to have died of natural causes."

"Recently?"

"Within the past couple of days. 2 men aged roughly 70 and 50 and 2 women aged about 80 and 40. As I say, I'll have more for you soon."

DI Revie had a look at the open coverings surrounding the bodies and agreed how professional they all looked. They all appeared to be naked and clean and looked quite fresh corpses.

"Any clues around the mortuary?" he asked.

"Not that we've found yet, but it's difficult when it's so dark. You didn't see anything on your trip before you found the bodies? I gather you were on some kind of ghost hunt?"

"Not a ghost hunt. A hunt for criminal damagers – if there's such a word."

"Did you find either?"

"No."

The friends parted and Revie and Hughes walked towards the church, where the bulk of the officers were congregating. As he crossed the road, he noticed that there were members of the public walking towards him.

"Get them out of the way," he urged Hughes.

"Sir, sir, I need to speak to you!" shouted one of the men.

"Speak to one of my officers!" he shouted back.

"No. You are the one in charge. I want to see if the bodies are my parents. My name is Gary Townsend."

"Should I know that name?"

"You might want to know who I am when you start trying to identify the bodies."

"Then one of the officers will take your details. Constable!" Revie beckoned to a uniform standing near to him. "Take the details of Mr Townsend."

"Sir."

"Let me see the bodies now. Let me see if it's my parents."

"What makes you think your parents are here and dead at that?"

Gary obviously drunk, rushed the DI but was caught by the constable and thrown to the ground before he reached him.

"Fucking get off me!" he yelled.

"I have enough on my hands this evening Mr Townsend and so I suggest you go home after giving the officer your contact details. Wait there until we call you. We are not allowing you on the site and I will have you arrested if you do not go home right now."

Gary Townsend rubbed his face and got up from the road. His brother Stephen had arrived and began helping him up.

"Is it them?" he asked.

"They won't let me see," he answered.

The brothers took more persuading to leave the area, however they moved more quickly when at the same time around 20 Special Constables arrived and were sent on duty around the perimeter of the hospital grounds by walking through the numerous lanes and fields and pushing intruders out. They took details of everyone they saw and listened to gossip as they followed them to the boundary walls. Reporting back at debrief, they told of ghosts stories and phantoms and if the bodies were the Townsends, it was the sons who had killed them.

DI Revie ordered a thorough search of the hospital and the grounds to commence at 8 am the following morning. The ACC had called into the station to speak to him at 6 am. Revie had managed two hours sleep on the bench seat in one of the interview rooms. He looked rough, but promised to have a wash and brush up before the public saw him.

"I'm leaving you in charge of this John, so don't let me down. A good result should gildy up your promotion. I want DCI Revie in my team." ACC John Ryan knew this was a promotion John Revie desired and he had only held it back for personal and selfish reasons. He wasn't going to let him know that – not yet.

"Thank you sir. I'm hoping that the case will be solved easily. It's crazy enough. There is a search beginning this morning inside and out and the PM's are due later this afternoon. They are taking photos of the faces, nothing too horrible there and these will be shown to any officer who has not yet seen them. If we have no luck there, we will speak to the gawkers from last night."

"I hear that the Townsends were making a particular fuss."

"Yes sir. I'm going to interview them myself this morning. I've spoken to the Tresaiths and they would say nothing without a lawyer. I'll leave them for a day and let them stew a bit."

"Not too much on the stewing, Revie. Philip and John are - associates of mine."

"I will do my job. That's what I am paid to do."

*

The search of the grounds found nothing out of the ordinary. They found rubbish either blown in or deposited by supposed vandals. There were no piles of cigarette ends or pieces of cloth matching the swaddled bodies. There were no drag marks or tyre marks not accounted for by police or caretaker. Every room within the hospital had been searched thoroughly and there was no sign of habitation by neither man nor ghost.

The bodies were recognised by no one in the force and the PM's showed that they had died of pneumonia. They had all been treated with antibiotics and sympathy according to the pathologist, but had succumbed as any patient in a hospital might have done. "It is as though we have gone back in time and collected bodies when patients were at the hospital – but naturally, that is not possible," he said to Gwen when she witnessed the post mortems.

"But someone put them there and did it carefully. Maybe something will show up with the DNA," she answered.

"If we have someone to check it against."

Speaking to DI Revie on the phone when she got back in the car, they decided to meet at the Townsend yard.

"I've spoken to Gary and he says he and his two brothers will be at their office waiting for us. Should be an interesting meeting," he told her.

"I will be there in half an hour," she told him. "I'll wait in the car park, boss."

As it turned out, her boss was already there, talking on the phone. He finished the call and walked over to her.

"That was the Tresaith solicitor. Apparently they are ready to talk to us this afternoon at his office in Caernarfon."

"Are we going?"

"No time today and I'm not running round after that family. I've told them we can see them at the station in the morning."

"Bet that pleased them."

"Not particularly. Now, I don't know whether these Townsends have anything to tell us and why they think their parents are the bodies."

"Well we'll know soon, won't we?"

They were shown into a large office by a young and very sexy blonde girl. She wore high heels and a short skirt and John imagined that she caused quite a rumpus when she walked across the haulage yard.

"This is DI Revie and Miss, err, forgotten her name."

"My name is DS Hughes."

"Thank you for coming, both of you. We would have come in to the station, but perhaps it's easier to see us here. Less drama," said Andrew.

"Would you like some tea or coffee? Or perhaps something stronger?" asked Gary.

"Nothing thanks," answered DI Revie.

"Well I'm having one." The three brothers took bottles of beer from the fridge which stood in the corner of the office.

DI Revie took out the photographs he had and handed them across the desk. They watched the reactions of each of the brothers as they looked at the pictures. They looked curious and surprised.

"Do you recognise any of these people?" he asked.

They each answered in the negative, but kept hold of the pictures.

"Why did you think it was your parents?" DS Hughes enquired.

"Because we haven't seen either of them since they went in to the asylum twenty five years ago," said Gary.

"According to our records, they both died," said DI Revie. "We haven't been idle since last night. In fact you have all presented their death certificates as evidence to allow you to take over all the businesses. You three men are all rich because of the documentation and statements you have made to that end."

"We did, but we were paying the Tresaith family to keep them both out of the public eye at the asylum. We did it for their own good."

"And what happened to your parents after the place closed down?" asked Hughes.

"They kept looking after them and we kept paying." Stephen seemed to be talking for all of them.

"Why would they do that and where would they do that?" said Revie.

"Still at the asylum and they were doing it for the money. A lot of money and we aren't the only ones. There are lots of patients still there."

"I don't understand where the patients would be, we have searched the place more than once and there are no patients there."

"They must be hiding them somewhere. We are still paying them."

"How does this payment occur? Is it cash or through your bank?" Revie was still deciding whether they were lying to him or not.

"It used to be through the bank and now we pay cash."

"Where is this cash payment made?" Hughes was beginning to think that they were getting close to a useful revelation.

"Our secretary takes the money to their secretary."

"Why do you keep paying if you think your parents may be dead?"

"The Tresaiths are blackmailing us about it. It's all getting ridiculous," Andrew sounded depressed. "And it's costing us a shedload of money."

"I would like you to put that all in a statement for me, Mr Townsend. All of you. Can you come to the station and do that for us? There are a lot of serious allegations there and I would like to have as much information as possible. In the meantime, can you let me know who else has family members at the hospital?"

Andrew Townsend appeared to be going to tell DI Revie, but a hand on his shoulder from Gary stopped him from proceeding.

"We'll get in touch with our solicitor and have him come with us. He will make an appointment with your officers."

CHAPTER TEN

"How many of them have actually arrived?" DI Revie had just been informed that the Tresaith solicitor was in the interview room.

"Philip and John Tresaith, plus Mr Acland the solicitor. He's one of those London solicitors."

"I thought they were bringing their man from Caernarfon?"

"You'd think so wouldn't you? Perhaps they need a fancier solicitor for some reason."

"Thanks Sergeant, we'll be there shortly."

"Wonder why the change of solicitor?" asked DS Hughes.

"Guaranteed it's something ropey."

They walked through the white corridors decorated with boards full of notices. Some advertised items for sale, some rooms for rent, others sports tournaments. The public were not allowed in these corridors. Downstairs in the interview room there was only a notice informing the public not to drink and drive. Reading it were the Tresaith brothers while their solicitor sat at the desk, pulling papers out of his briefcase.

"Thank you for coming in," Revie said to the three men.

"My name is Clarence Acland and I am the solicitor for the Tresaith family. You may direct your questions through me. We also acknowledge that my clients are not under arrest and may leave at any time."

"I have never inferred that your clients are under arrest. Indeed, all we are doing is clarifying what has been happening at Tresaith hospital."

"It is no longer a hospital. It closed ten years ago with all patients leaving to go to other hospitals."

"And none of the patients or staff remained?" asked DI Revie.

"None of the patients. The last one left in June 1995 and some staff remained to clean up the place and remove drugs and similar paraphernalia. Currently there is only a caretaker, whom I believe you have already met. He works there in return for grazing rights."

"I have met him and he kindly showed me around the place so that I could check on the trespassing which has been occurring. That's how we found the bodies."

"So I gather," said the solicitor. "But my clients know nothing about that."

"Mr Tresaith, either of you will do. I have information that your family have been taking payments for patients who were not officially on the books, so to speak. And that this has continued through the years since the closure."

The brothers began to speak, "Don't be so idiotic! Why and how would we do such a thing?"

"My clients wish to make clear that allegations such as these are fabricated and frivolous." He glared at his clients, who lowered their eyes and became quiet.

"Who has made these allegations specifically?" he asked.

"That I cannot say at present, but the allegation refers to Mr and Mrs Townsend."

"So it's that lot. They are always causing trouble."

"Philip!" said Mr Acland. "I suggest that you search the hospital thoroughly and there you will find nothing and no one. You will find nothing to connect my client to these unfortunate people."

"How do you know that sir? You haven't seen the pictures?"

"Whoever they are, they have nothing to do with their demise. We will look at the pictures, however."

DI Revie pushed the pictures across the desk and the three men looked at them with great interest and lack of recognition. The brothers Tresaith seemed almost relieved as they pushed the pictures back.

"I don't know who they are," said Philip.

"They look very peaceful," said John Tresaith. "Was it murder?"

"We don't know yet. You have never seen these people before? You are sure of that?"

"If my clients say they do not know who these unfortunates are, then they don't know how they are," confirmed the solicitor.

DI Revie picked up the photographs and banged them on the table as he rearranged them back into a neat pile. He smiled at the men as he did this and they smiled nervously back.

"I would like to talk to your sister too. Selina isn't it? She was the last Superintendent I believe."

"Miss Tresaith is not currently in the country, I'm afraid. She is in Canada," Mr Acland informed them. He was putting his papers back into the briefcase, signalling to the group that the meeting was coming to an end.

"But Sarah Tresaith is not? I would like to speak to her at some point," Revie persisted.

"I will arrange that for you, Detective Inspector. She is feeling under the weather currently. Her doctor has recommended complete rest."

"Thank you for coming in today. I will let you know when we have finished at the hospital. I would imagine that it will be a few days yet." Revie and Hughes got up from their seats and Hughes opened the door. Revie wanted to end the meeting himself.

*

"They are all hiding stuff boss. I'm thinking that the Townsends were nearer the truth in what they were telling us," said Gwen Hughes.

"You think that they have a secret group of patients that they have squirreled away somewhere? Why?"

"For a start, Roy Townsend was a couple of days short of getting arrested for rape and murder, when he vanished. He was declared dead after 7 years and the sons inherited," said Gwen.

"What's the reason for the wife vanishing?"

"She was starting to go senile and perhaps they were frightened she would talk."

"That leaves us with the Tresaiths running a hospital illegally. That's a hell of a risk for them."

"Perhaps we ought to check it out though? Why have the Townsends suddenly come up with this story?"

"Don't know. I suggest that for the next day, uniform ask around about rumours similar and then a couple of us go and check the hospital out one night while no one else is about."

"Like a ghost hunt you mean."

"Maybe, I'm not really sure how else to approach this one."

*

They managed to arrange the investigation three nights later after most of the official searching had been completed. They did not inform the Tresaiths or the Townsends, only their own officers. Revie did not want to raise suspicion or encourage any evidence to be tampered with. No one locally had recognised the pictures and had nothing to say in regard to hidden patients. Many had worked at the site, most had several family members who had worked there in some capacity and yet none would admit to knowing about anyone other than the official medical list.

"If we find nothing tonight, we have no more leads to follow," said Revie, unusually mournfully.

"You're giving up a bit quick boss. Not like you."

"I have a weird feeling about this one Hughes. I can't put my finger on it, because I haven't been able to reconcile what is going on here with anything I've come across before."

"And you've come across a lot boss?"

Revie looked at his sergeant and half smiled, "I have indeed Hughes. Wrap up warm tonight and bring more than one torch in case one fails. Even I don't fancy being there without a light. It was creepy as fuck in the daylight when all I had to do was follow around an old man who knew where he was going. I don't fancy getting lost."

"To be fair, neither do I. But in case we do, I'm bringing sandwiches and a flask, boss."

They were dropped off by a patrol car outside the main gate at 11pm. They were given instructions to be back there at 3 am and if they weren't there, to come in and find them.

"And come back very quick if either one of us shouts for help," said Gwen as she shuffled out of the back seat.

The uniforms laughed at her, but she said, "I mean it! The more I think of this, the more spooked I am!"

"If you don't want the station knowing that you are nothing but a big girl, you will lead the way into this spooky mansion," encouraged Revie.

Tresaith Asylum certainly did look like a spooky mansion once the car left them. They jumped over the stone wall and stood up to look at the skyline of the place.

"It's just like a movie set," noticed DI Revie. "Like a Hammer Horror film set."

"Boss, is you keep this up, I may have to complain about harassment from a superior officer."

"What kind of harassment?"

"Trying to make me cry and run away! But I warn you, I'm not going to."

In answer to their musings, a bolt of lightning cracked the sky above the asylum. This was followed by a long thunder roll.

"Great, now it's going to piss down," said Hughes pulling her anorak hood over her head.

"We should maintain radio and mouth silence from now on Hughes. We don't want to disturb anyone unnecessarily until we know what's going on here."

"Ok boss." DS Hughes had great respect for the boss, in spite of the banter.

The lightning was the only way they could see where they were walking but it did mean they did not need to turn on their torches. DI Revie kept glancing at the building while hoping not to see any lights or spooky figures there. In spite of being a 15 year veteran on the force, this was one of those times when he didn't want to find anything. But he wasn't going to let Gwen know. It was fine so far though, nothing unusual – if he discounted the four dead bodies.

"I think that this is the front door key," he said to Hughes handing her the large brass object.

"It's as though everything is a set piece here, isn't it? We joked about the Hammer Horror thing, but seriously…" Hughes had stopped mid turn and looked around. The night was as black as black until the lightning struck. Then a rainy, blurry scene in black and white met their eyes. The lodge house was vaguely visible and its inset windows took what light was available during the flash and highlighted its Gothic architecture.

"It is, but let's not allow that to alarm us. We have a job to do. Are you still happy to carry on? It's not too late for you to back out?"

"And let the team say the woman can't hack it? I have enough to put up with as it is, with talk of tampons and knitting."

"Really? They still talk like that to you? I thought everyone knew better."

"Most do boss. There are some idiots about though."

"Names?"

"No boss. But if you hear that Sgt. Gwen Hughes has laid out a couple of fellow officers – well there will be your names right there!"

The key turned and the pair went into the lobby. Revie thought how fucking creepy previously very busy buildings were when they were empty. He had had to deal with a murder at a railway station once and when they closed the crime scene down and most of the investigative team had left, Revie almost had a panic attack. The atmosphere seemed to fill with the dead as soon as the living left.

They had previously agreed to check out each room and act as though there were residents and staff still there. That way they would remember to keep quiet and stealthy. Each room was checked as they went in and quickly scouted around, but there was nothing. Uniform and forensics had been everywhere and found nothing - there was nothing. And yet the further they went into the hospital, the more it seemed that they were being watched. Revie noticed the sound of his boots on the wooden floor echoing down the hallways. Gwen's trainers were not making the same impact and he couldn't hear her footsteps. The storm had calmed down now and when Revie looked out of the window he could see and hear only light rain. It was very cold though, too cold for the time of year. Maybe it was just the old, damp building he could feel. He was in the Medical Superintendent's office and he wondered why both of the doctors in charge had gone to Canada. Had they gone together? When did they go? He would get someone to find that out tomorrow. He pulled out cabinet drawers and found them empty of everything except for a few pieces of paper. He sifted idly through them and noted that they were torn edges from a ledger of some sort. Hughes walked in on him and whispered that she had checked her rooms and found nothing. Revie put the pieces of paper into his pocket and followed her out of the offices. As they did there was the sound of footsteps seemingly in the corridor. They stopped in their tracks and turned off their head torches.

Peeping around the office door, there was a sense that people were walking down it and going about their daily business. No one was there naturally. Revie felt suddenly cold, as though a freezer door had opened in front of them. Goose pimples and hair rising from their skin, Gwen almost forgot to breathe.

"What the fuck is that?" she hissed.

"I expect this is the point where I should give you a perfectly logical explanation – only I can't think of one," he answered.

The invisible but noisy footsteps echoed down the corridor and stopped as the first ward door was reached. A creaking noise followed although the door did not move and the footsteps faded away.

"Actual fucking ghosts," muttered Gwen.

Revie reached into his pocket and pulled out his warrant card and showed it to her.

"Professionals," he said.

She nodded and they walked through the ward doors and followed the now vanished sound of footsteps. They walked a little closer together than was usual for two officers of the law.

The wards were the same as had been on Revie's previous visit. Beds lined neatly, head to the wall and most surrounded by closed curtains or curtain screens. It was more than disconcerting to flash their headlights from one side of the room to the other. DS Hughes tugged lightly on her boss's coat and pointed at one of the screened beds. He looked where she pointed and made out what he thought was a patient in one of the beds. He realised that he was only able to see it as there was some light source behind the screen. And that shouldn't be so.

"Do we go closer?" asked Hughes.

"Yes, we must," said her boss and walked calmly towards the screen. This he swept back and there lying on the bed was an elderly lady dressed in a calico nightgown and wearing leather slippers. She looked very old – very old indeed. She opened her eyes and looked at them. They looked back at her and she vanished.

"Boss? Fuck. What's going on here?"

"I would say that this place is haunted and that might explain the strange lights and noises locals have heard. It cannot explain the four deaths and for that reason alone, I'm not sure that we should mention what we've seen to anyone else."

"I'm actually beginning to wonder if we will get out of here to speak to any fucker about anything boss."

"We might as well carry on, we are half way through the place and its only midnight."

"And no one's coming unless we scream."

"Exactly. Ssshhh."

They were now so close that they were touching arms and neither made a move away. Pure fear kept them close, nothing remotely sexual. The footsteps had started up again, definitely a woman's feet, wearing low heels. At least they were walking away again and the two took up their police roles, straightened their backs and followed the footsteps. They led out into the corridor and towards a large staircase. Revie knew from his previous trip that it was made from oak and beautiful. The footsteps ran lightly up the stairs and then turned left at the top. A door opened and closed and the sounds stopped.

"There has to be a rational explanation."

"Tell me what it is then boss. I haven't got a fucking clue."

The thunderstorm had a new lease of life and light flashed in through the windows every few minutes. The thunder rolls were terrific and although the effects added to the spookiness of the night, it spurred them on to complete their duties. They didn't follow the footsteps, but continued through the wards checking the beds and the cupboards. Although they both felt as though each ward were full of nurses and patients, there were no visuals and remarkably they began to become used to the sensations.

The icy rain continued throughout their walks but there were no actual physical sightings. The ghosts were just round the corner, just out of sight, out of experience. The pair knew they were following ghosts, but what to do? Run and hide or carry on? The latter would at least get them to the back door pretty quickly.

Subsequently the second half of the investigation was completed much more quickly than the first. They trotted through the kitchens, laundry room and bathrooms. They checked for hidden doors, staircases and cupboards and everything was as it should be. They finally reached the main back door and Revie unlocked it.

"Only the courtyard stables and garages to look at now, Hughes. Then its home."

"I can't say I'm sorry about that boss."

They pulled open the door, which seemed jammed and required that both of them use their strength on it. When it finally opened, they were hit by a wave of cold rain, thunder and lightning all at the same time. The lightning lit the yard for almost four seconds and in that time they noticed several people scurrying from one side of the courtyard to the other.

"Was that ghosts or real people?" asked DS Hughes.

Revie shone his hand torch and directed his head torch across the yard but there was no longer anyone to see. A thorough check of the building from which the figures left and entered was made, but yet again nothing. It was 2.10 and DI Revie said that they should walk round to the front of the asylum and meet the other officers.

"Round and not through boss? Please?"

He grinned and they walked along the lanes, past the mortuary and the church and the nurses' home. The avenue of trees which led from the asylum to the home rustled in front and behind them, adding to the terrifying atmosphere of the experience. They walked across the fields, over the wall and to the squad car which was waiting for them.

"Find what you wanted sir?" asked one.

"Didn't find anything to speak of," Revie said as he climbed in the back of the car.

"Oh. We thought you must have found something and got some back up."

"What makes you think that?"

The constable jabbed his finger in the direction of the asylum. There were lights moving around the top floor.

"Drive on Jackson," instructed the DI.

CHAPTER ELEVEN

"I need to tell you something about what happened last night," said DS Hughes as she sat opposite DI Revie at 11 the next morning.

"It was you doing all the ghostly effects?"

"No boss. But the old lady on the bed, you know the one who vanished."

"Hard to forget."

"Yes, I know. Only the thing is…"

"I have other things to do Hughes."

"Yes sir. Only, I think she was my great grandmother."

This statement certainly got Revie's attention and he put down his pen and tipped his fingers together before pressing them against his mouth. The habit was recognised by those who knew him well as an indication he was trying to appear professional, while hiding frustration that the information had not been brought to his attention earlier.

"Your grandmother."

"No, great grandmother. You see, I thought she looked familiar, but then I thought no way, she's supposed to be dead. That's what we were told anyway by my mother. She was supposed to have some sort of mental problems, like she beat my Nain a lot and was supposed to have poisoned my Taid. But he didn't die and they put her in the asylum and then she died. So this morning I rang Mam and she said that she thought her Nain had died at the asylum but she couldn't remember because she hadn't gone to a funeral. But she definitely looked like her."

"Did you tell your mother about last night?"

"No boss, of course not, I just said I was thinking of doing some family research and that was one of the stories I remembered. Anyway, I went round to her house before I came in and got this photograph." Hughes handed over a grainy snap of an elderly couple. Revie took it from her and looked at it carefully.

"It does look like her, I'll give you that. But seriously, how old would she be?"

"She was born 1892 according to Mam, so in theory she should be dead or not far off dead by now. She would be 113"

"And taking all of that into consideration, why would she be lying on a bed in an abandoned asylum?"

"I know and why would she vanish before our eyes?"

While they pondered this conundrum, ACC Ryan walked into the office.

"How is the investigation progressing? I gather you went on a night-time prowl at the hospital last night?"

"We did sir, but turned up nothing I'm afraid."

"A waste of police resources would you say?"

"No sir, all information we collect or eliminate helps us out I would say."

"Make sure that you don't waste any more money DI Revie, we have to answer to accounts with everything these days. Do we have any leads?"

"No sir, but we are going to Tresaith Manor this afternoon. We have a warrant."

"Yes I saw that. Be careful with the family, we can't be seen to be harassing them."

"Not harassment sir. It would have been better for them if they had helped us a little more without the warrant. But I do need to eliminate them, the bodies were found on their property."

"Understood Revie, but none of your bombastic approaches here please, I don't want the family upset. They have a lot of connections." He left the room and DS Hughes stared at him as he left.

"Why should connections make a difference? To the law, I mean?"

"They shouldn't. They don't. We do our job."

At 3 pm they were knocking at the front door of the Manor. Revie and Hughes were accompanied by three uniformed officers and three special constables. John Tresaith seemed unperturbed that they were there and stood aside as they entered his home.

"Please do not make a mess, officers. We keep a tidy house here and if there is any damage caused, I shall sue you." Addressing Revie he added, "I already told you that these poor people are nothing to do with us and so I am surprised to find you here. However, we will cooperate with you. Please also be aware that there are CCTV cameras in every room which are currently recording everything going on."

DI Revie thanked him and then beckoned his team to split into the previously agreed groups and conduct the investigation. They dispersed without speaking, for they had all heard about the cameras. There would be no joking around.

The Tresaith family, John, Philip and Sarah sat in the drawing room, drinking tea and reading. They ignored everything that was happening at their home and dealt with any questions when required. DI Revie walked from one floor to another of the spacious stone house and inwardly admired the traditional architecture and décor. It was plainly obvious that this property had been inhabited by several generations of the same family.

While walking the top floor alone he noticed a young girl looking at him from a doorway. She beckoned him over.

It was Carys Tresaith.

She put her finger to her lips and had him follow her into the room. It appeared to be a servants room no longer occupied.

"There are no cameras in here Mr Revie. There are none on this landing either, so the family will not have seen you speak to me."

"I'm not so sure that it is a good idea that I do speak to you Miss Tresaith. Not only are you a child, but I have been told not to speak to you."

"From my uncles and aunt you mean? They aren't my parents and I don't have to keep their stupid secrets."

"What stupid secrets and who are your parents?"

"My mother is Selina Tresaith and she has gone to Canada, to Saskatchewan to be specific, to try and get my father to come back here. Or perhaps to establish some sort of life in order that I may join them there. My uncles do not want this to happen and demand that I remain here on the family estates and go to the English schools that the Tresaiths have always attended. All of this is without asking my feelings on the matter."

Revie admired the young girl's maturity and asked her, "Do you know who your father is?"

Carys looked at him as though he was mad. "Naturally I know Mr Revie! I am neither a bastard nor a foundling. My father is my mother's husband, Lloyd Wright. He was

Medical Superintendent at the Asylum when mother was there. Surely you should know this?"

"I should know this, I didn't know this. Do you have contact with your father?"

"Some, not enough. My uncles don't like it, I'm afraid."

"That's unfortunate, it is important to know your father. Now, you mentioned secrets?"

"The patients at the asylum are the secrets. My family's wealth was originally built on the backs of men, women and children in Yorkshire mills and factories. Then that was added to with the money they made from the Asylum and the patients there. And some of those patients shouldn't have been there…"

"Inspector!" John Tresaith was standing behind them. He was absolutely furious.

"Carys, please leave us now. Go to your room!"

"My dear Uncle John, I must tell you that I sought out the Inspector and tried to speak to him. He did not ask me anything and all I have told him are my parents' names. I do not expect to hear that Inspector Revie has been complained about. Thank you Inspector for treating me like a grown up, I appreciate that." Carys walked away.

"She is correct. Mr Tresaith. I did not know that she was on this floor and I did not seek her out."

"I must ask that you do not speak to my niece without someone else being present."

"An appropriate adult? I do know the rules. However, currently I do not need to speak to Miss Tresaith. I will let you know if that changes."

John Tresaith stood aside and allowed Revie to pass.

*

"Do you think that she was going to tell you something else?" asked DS Hughes as they drove back from the Manor.

"Possibly, she seems to dislike her current guardians and she is a very mature young lady. What she did tell me could be read two ways."

"Yes boss. And we found nothing at the Manor?"

"It seems not. We appear to be good at finding nothing in this case."

"Except for ghosts and spirits," joked Hughes. "I keep trying to make a rational explanation for all of that. I mean, we have to be careful not to miss something relevant while we are pretending we haven't seen any ghosts."

"I appear to have taught you well."

"You have boss. Look, now is as good a time to say this, but I'm thinking of going to university, so that I can study law properly"

"Leave the force you mean?"

"Yes. I wanted to tell you before, but I wasn't sure that I'd get in. But I have and I am going to be the best lawyer there is."

"Well I'm very impressed and pleased for you. When do you leave?"

"I have my notice with me, I've had it for about a week but was trying to find the right time to ask you - tell you. So I suppose this is my notice, but I have holidays and time in lieu, so I've only got a week to go."

DI Revie looked across at her, "I shall miss you DS Hughes, your cheery disposition on the early mornings..."

"And my dead Nain late at night."

"Indeed. I know that you will be on hand to help us with that even after you leave."

"Last night made me realise that I would rather be on the theory side and not the practical. It's been great, but I won't miss it."

*

They held the leaving party for Gwen at the Conservative Club at Tresaith because they were owed a favour. It all went well with plenty of drink, food and loud music. Gwen really let her hair down and before her evening was over was being helped by two of her female ex colleagues to throw up in the ladies.

Almost three weeks had passed since the bodies had been found and they were no further forward than they had been at the beginning of the investigation. The Townsends had completely shut down and were only speaking through their solicitor, citing stress as their reason. They did not appreciate the townspeople talking about prisoner patients being kept at the remains of the asylum. As DI Revie had neither new evidence nor reason to interview them, he had left them alone. He had patience enough and when something turned up, as he was convinced it would, he would talk to them then.

Today the new DS was arriving at the station. He was a Scot who had recently worked in Caernarfon and wanted to move because he thought it would help his promotional prospects. Colin Buchanan had plenty of promotional aspiration. Now divorced and free to concentrate on his career, he was focussed in his desires for success.

Plus, he was more than interested in this conundrum at Tresaith and wanted in.

The team nodded and smiled at him upon his arrival and the women beamed. DS Buchanan was a good looking man. DI Revie welcomed him and beckoned him to sit down.

"DS Buchanan, I have some good reports about you. You were particularly helpful with The Red Gable case, I'm told."

"That was in retrospect sir. That case actually happened in the 1976 and was quite famous. A retired Navy man apparently went mad and killed four people and then himself. That's how it was written up anyway. There was some new evidence a couple of years back and I got a bit obsessed with it."

"I recognise work obsession. I have a bit of that myself. Did you solve the mystery?"

"No sir. But I have a lot of ideas and some of them lead back to Tresaith. I was investigating this new evidence – in my own time and then this transfer came up."

"And so here you are. Perhaps you can share your thoughts if you find they are relevant to the cases we have ongoing. Tresaith Asylum isn't the only one."

"I understand sir. I'm not afraid of work."

"You're Scottish."

"Yes sir. Not a problem is it?"

"Of course not, my mother was a Scot."

"She sounds lovely sir," smiled Buchanan.

"She was. I want you to get some stories together about patients you can find who stayed at the hospital and were not seen again. I know it's a big job, but it might help the team get a new perspective on a case that's going nowhere. Present it to us on Friday, give you time to settle in."

"Ok sir."

CHAPTER TWELVE

DI Revie was impressed with his new bagman. His main focus appeared to be the job and he was able to research cases that were no longer being researched by the force itself. A scan through his records showed that he was also keeping on top of his allocated work. Perhaps that was why he was recently divorced. He had asked for a tour around the Asylum, preferably at night in order to get a better view of the problem. Revie wanted to say no, but instead said,

"Do you want company? I've been there twice already, but perhaps you ought to take another officer with you."

"DC Brake has said he will come with me. He's interested, so I thought we would go tomorrow night. That way I am not missing any detective time," he grinned.

"Make sure you radio base in and out. We need to know where you are at all times."

"Expecting trouble guv?"

"Not really. But that hospital is a maze and there is no power there and sometimes there are yobbos drinking and being idiots. Right, now we are going to interview these Townsend boys again. You haven't met them yet, so keep your eyes and ears open."

Their discussion was interrupted by the aforementioned Brake.

"Hi. I've just heard back from our oppos in Canada - Saskatchewan."

"Tell me."

"Dr. Lloyd Wright has been working in Prince Albert at a hospital for 8 years. He's a Canadian citizen now, but there is no sign of Selina Tresaith. In fact there are no records of her leaving this country ever. She doesn't even have a passport."

"That's interesting."

"Plus boss. I checked on the girl Carys Tresaith and she has been registered as Selina's daughter, but the father is not recorded."

"Thanks for that Brake. You've done well. Anything else?"

"No boss. Well, only that I would be happy to visit the Asylum with DS Buchanan, if that's ok with you?"

"We've just been discussing it Brake. Seems we all fancy having a look round there."

Brake was honest. "My mum was a nurse there and my Taid worked in the mortuary, so I'm really keen to get in there and have a look."

"Did you go there as a child? With your mum?"

Brake said he had.

"Did you speak to them about the case?"

"No boss! My Taid is dead now, but I don't talk about cases, really."

"OK. OK. But I don't mind if you have a word with her about anything unusual she remembers from her time there. Presumably she saw the pictures of the bodies?"

"I didn't show her, but a uniform did a house to house. She didn't know who they were."

"Thanks Brake." Revie turned to Buchanan and said, "Come on. Off we go."

*

This time they went to Townsend Towers, as it was known in the town. The gaudy building was actually called Plas Cerrig and had started life as a gentleman's residence on the outskirts of Tresaith. Built of grey stone it had stood in testament to classical beauty for 250 years. That was until the Townsends had bought it from a poverty stricken owner, the last in the line of Gruffydds who had owned it since the beginning. The Townsends steadily turned it into a horrendous circus like house, the kind you imagine someone with loads of money and no class would build.

The door was opened by a grim looking young woman whom Revie seemed to remember seeing at the garage.

"We've come to see any of the Townsend brothers," said Buchanan.

"Fuck all to do with me," she answered. "I'm not the maid." She flung open the door and ran past them before jumping into an Astra which she wheel span out of the drive.

No one else came to the door, so the men let themselves in. The hallway was empty, but a door to one of the rooms off, was open. They walked towards it quietly, not suspiciously in order to better hear the conversation which was going on there at a raised level.

"Those fucking coppers will be here soon," said Gary.

"Are you going to tell them this time?" asked Stephen.

"We can't prove anything," said Andrew.

"Can't prove that they are still alive?"

"They have been declared dead officially."

"Still no bodies," Gary sounded pleased.

"No one is likely to find any, are they?" Andrew seemed to walking towards the door. Revie decided now would be a good time to make themselves known.

"Ah Mr Townsend, a young woman let us in and then drove off," he walked into the room and was met by three surprised faces.

"How long have you been out there?" asked Gary.

"Long enough to hear that you all seem unsure about the life or death status of your parents."

"Have you found out who the bodies are yet?" Stephen seemed concerned.

"Not yet, I'm afraid. We wanted to have another word with you about your initial belief that two of them were your parents."

"Hysterics and alcohol Mr Revie," laughed Gary.

"We have never discovered what happened to our parents and so we had them declared dead through the solicitor after seven years. It was the only way we could keep the business going properly," said Andrew.

"What exactly happened when they vanished?" asked Buchanan. The brothers looked at him as though they had just seen him.

"Do I know you?" asked Andrew.

"I doubt it Mr Townsend, I don't know you. It would help us if you could tell us about it all."

The brothers looked at each other and Andrew spoke. "I'll tell them."

The police settled down on the sofas, hoping that they would get some proper information at last.

Andrew began, "If you've found anything out about my dad, you will know that he was a bullying, lying shit. He crossed all sorts of people in his time, most of the people round here, definitely. Mam was pretty good to us and to him, but he gave her a horrible time. He had affairs and kept her short of money and affection and let her work more hours than she should, while he fucked about and got pissed at the pub. It broke her mind in the end and about twenty years ago she went senile. She ended up in the hospital at Tresaith after he proper battered her and she just went downhill."

"She had begun to tell people about Dad's secrets," interrupted Stephen, "and there were plenty of those."

"So Dad didn't want her back out in the locality. Then suddenly he decided to go to the hospital too because he was suffering with his heart, or his lungs or some shit. He had been alright before and then suddenly he was gone. We had to pay massive bills to the Asylum for both of them, but they were never there when we called and the Tresaiths keep demanding money. We always pay but we think they must be dead. I mean, fuck, the place has been closed for nearly ten years."

"And where do you think the Tresaiths are keeping your parents if the place is closed?" asked Buchanan.

"Could be anywhere. Could be under their house or at one of their other places," said Gary.

"Where are the other places?"

"I believe they have an estate south of Caernarfon," interjected Buchanan.

The others looked at him and he smiled in response. "I had reason to know that from my time over there."

"Well it wouldn't surprise me if they are keeping loads of patients there."

"Do you have any proof whatsoever about this?" asked Revie.

"Only that there are lots of people missing if you start to look into it. Local people who haven't had a funeral and have just vanished could be there."

"Do you have any of the invoices they sent you from the Asylum?"

"No Inspector. We paid cash. They always wanted cash."

"Do you have any record at all of your parents being at the Asylum? Anyone who can verify your story?"

The brothers appeared stunned at this question and Andrew answered slowly, "It was all done pretty quietly to be honest. We didn't want to advertise the fact that Mam was a loony and Dad not far behind. A couple of people who worked for us at the time dealt with it all. But they are dead now, so there is no proof," said Gary.

"Except for our word," said Andrew.

"Hmmm. I see," answered Revie, his tone indicating that their word meant little to him. As he and the DS Buchanan were led out the front door again by Stephen, Revie asked,

"What do really believe happened to your parents Mr Townsend?"

"I don't know Mr Revie. My father made many enemies during his lifetime and my mother was an idiot. I don't just mean that she allowed Dad to be as crooked and abusive as he was, but I think she just avoided everything while knowing all about it."

"How does that make her an idiot?" asked Buchanan.

"Because she was in the perfect position to take advantage, while she was the signatory on all the accounts. Dad had been bankrupt twice and was never cleared. He relied on her for years and then he persuaded her to allow me Andrew and Gary to become signatories."

"Wasn't she very keen?"

"Not really, but this way two signatories were needed for everything and none of us ever backed what she wanted to do and we would back each other. I suppose it sounds a bit mean," he added as an afterthought.

The policemen did think it was mean, but nothing surprises policemen.

CHAPTER THIRTEEN

"It is so ironic that it was my generation and probably the one prior who stood up against racism and sexism in the workplace and elsewhere and we are now called bigots by a generation who have no concept of what it was like prior to the mid-eighties."

DS Buchanan was speaking to Gwladys Roberts, a middle aged woman who had worked as a young nurse at the hospital.

"Was there much sexism and racism at Tresaith?"

"Some. It was mainly when there was an older man in charge of a department, like the laundry or the gardens or somewhere. The sports departments were quite cruel too. Making comments about how the women dressed and particularly if they discovered that anyone was homosexual."

"I suppose there was a lot of abuse towards them?" asked Buchanan.

"I don't think so, not really. Perhaps there was in cities and such, but here it was more curiosity or amazement. And probably using inappropriate words, but I never saw any cruelty or anyone refusing to work with them. There were probably some words used that these days are considered a reason to lose your job. I don't mean the n word, that's terrible, some other words."

Buchanan didn't answer for a moment, deciding how far to push her. She had called the station and asked to speak to someone in charge as she had information about those bodies up at the Asylum. Mrs Roberts beat him to it however.

"So you will want to know what I know, so to speak."

"It would help."

"I worked at the asylum, although we were supposed to call it a hospital, but no one ever did – right up to the last day. I mean after the patients had all gone to other hospitals and that was a very sad time. There was crying and sadness and depression, mostly from the staff because we were all going to lose our jobs. The patients left in trickles and were pretty well drugged up by the time they left, so they didn't really notice."

"Yes, I see," he answered, although he didn't.

"And I was one of the very few who stayed until the place closed down proper. And do you know what the funny thing about it is?"

"No."

"They changed suppliers six months before they closed down and then ordered enough to last several years with a full hospital. Dr. Tresaith said it was because they had to buy in bulk in order to get the discounts. But how were they going to use that many medical supplies? In fact they changed the food supplier and the linen people too."

"It does seem unusual, but not necessarily suspicious. What happened with the staff?"

"They sacked everyone in the end. Most just quietly left as the patient numbers reduced until about – well six months before it closed, they had sacked so many people that they had to employ temps to see them through to the end."

"But you lasted?"

"Yes, I did. But do you know what I think happened?"

"I can't imagine."

"I think they forgot that I was one of the original staff and just kept me on in error. Everyone else was just a temp, as I said and so they didn't know I had been there years and I never told them. I needed the money you see. Still do really."

"And when all the patients left, did the staff leave then?"

"The very last patient went and I was dismissed I think a few days afterwards. We just had to clear up and leave as we always had, I gather it hasn't changed that much?"

"Apparently not," answered Buchanan. He was hoping to visit the asylum himself shortly.

"The caretaker stayed on, that was all and no doubt you heard all about the trespassers and the lights and all that rubbish?"

"Indeed I have."

"Well I think that some of the patients stayed on. You know, I don't think they were all sent to new hospitals. I couldn't tell you which ones now."

"Could you remember which patients if you tried?"

"Better than that, I have my old diary and journals. I kept them from my time there. They must be in the attic or perhaps the shed somewhere. I'm also sure that the Tresaiths will have detailed records. They won't have burnt everything, will they?"

"Do you think that you could let me see the journals please?" This was helpful news.

"I'll get my daughter to find them for you. I get asthmatic if I start routing around in the dust."

"The sooner the better Mrs Roberts, if you don't mind."

"Glad to be of help. It's been on my mind ever since, but I didn't tell anyone. It seemed a bit daft and no one else had mentioned it. To be honest, I didn't really mention that I had been kept on that extra six months. I would have been called out. Lots of people were in financial trouble after losing their jobs and – well I just kept quiet."

DS Buchanan got up to leave.

"Thanks Mrs Roberts. Shall I call in tomorrow?"

"You can if you like. But I might just send our Gwenny over with it. I get tired so easily these days. I'm almost 60 you know!"

"Goodness, you don't look it," was all he could think of saying. Jeez, he hoped he looked a fucking sight better than her at 60.

*

When he got back to the station, DI Revie was in his office behind a closed door. He was talking to his computer.

"You have to go in, but quietly," said DC Parry. "He's Skyping Canada."

"OK," said Buchanan. He went in quietly and Revie smiled as he came in.

"DS Buchanan has just entered my office and so will be listening to us Dr. Wright."

Buchanan sat in the chair behind Revie and raised his hand. Dr Wright was 46, he knew that from looking through his records. He was a good looking man, but seemed a little strained.

"I haven't seen Dr Tresaith since the place closed. 1995 that was, but I'm sure you know that."

Buchanan noticed that Dr. Wright was flicking his gaze beyond his computer screen and he wondered who was with him. He didn't ask as he had been given no instructions to interfere.

"I have information that Carys is your daughter."

"Who told you that?"

"The information turned up during our enquiries. Is it true?"

"It is true, but no one is supposed to know that she is my daughter. Selina didn't want anyone to know."

"I think Carys knows," said Revie.

"How? Why? When did you see her?"

"I can't talk about that now. Why would Dr. Tresaith want to keep this information quiet? To what end?"

"She said it was to protect her, but I think it was really so I didn't take her to Canada with me."

"She thought you would kidnap her?"

"I don't know Mr Revie, Selina could be very awkward. I haven't spoken to her for years and I have nothing to do with my daughter. I am rather hoping that she will want to meet me and have a relationship once she no longer needs permission from her mother."

"We have also heard that Tresaith Hospital had several paying patients who were not on the regular roll call and were private cash patients. And some of these patients remained after the place closed down."

"I can't help you there. All the patients I saw were recorded with the Health Authority and accounted for if that's what you mean. As to patients remaining afterwards, I don't see how that could have happened, for the reasons I just stated."

"Do you know why suppliers were changed in the months prior to the hospital closure." Revie asked the questions in response to notes passed to him from his Sergeant.

Lloyd looked momentarily surprised but answered, "I don't know about all the suppliers, but I think some were changed because we had to order so far ahead with the regular suppliers. The new suppliers only needed a week or so's notice. When the patients were being moved, we couldn't plan that far in advance."

"We have been told that Dr. Tresaith is abroad, perhaps Canada. Do you know anything about that?"

Lloyd Wright looked thoughtful. "No! If she is in Canada, it's nowhere near me. As I said I have nothing to do with any of the Tresaith family and haven't for years. I cannot help you any further. Look, I'm going to have to go now, I have patients to see. My office opens at 9."

Revie looked at his watch, "Yes I see. It's 3 in the afternoon here. I will let you get on. I may want to speak to again."

"Fine," answered Lloyd and cut the connection before Revie could say anything else.

"Do you believe him?" asked Buchanan.

"No, I don't, but we can't make him come back here. When are you going back to the asylum?"

"Tonight I was thinking. Have you changed your mind? Will you come with me? I'm taking the Jones twins and Brake with me. They all volunteered." He knew, they all knew, that the visit of Revie and Hughes had been unusual even though neither had mentioned what had happened.

"With that kind of back up, how can I resist?"

This time they began the visit at 8 pm while it was still light. They arrived in two cars and parked them outside the main entrance. They had informed the caretaker what they were doing and he had expressed firstly surprise and then trepidation. Buchanan told him they were going anyway and that he should bring the keys to the station. This, he had done and Buchanan pulled the keys from his pocket and opened the main door. He was followed by Revie, Brake and the Jones brothers – called thus because of their names and nothing else. They were PC Sally Jones and PC Robert Jones and were no relation to each other.

The door slid open easily and the group went in.

"Gwen was right boss, this is a very creepy place. I came in here as a little girl with my mum in the eighties and this foyer was full of people going back and forth. It was such an interesting place. It's such a shame how it's ended up," said SJ.

"Did she? My mum worked here too. She worked as a tailoress though in one of the buildings out the back. She used to make her own clothes and also her friend's stuff. She's really good at it still. I think she probably used the material bought by the hospital anyway," answered RJ.

"I don't want to hear about using company equipment for private use!" shouted Revie.

"Do you think she will make me a dress? Only I've seen this one in a magazine and there is no way I can afford it," asked SJ.

"Sure. I'll ask her, better still she's over for Sunday lunch this week, come and meet her."

"When you two have finished organising your private lives, I would be grateful if you concentrate on the job in hand," said Buchanan.

"Sarge," they said in unison.

"Now, I want you two to cover the top two floors. Check for any hidden room by looking for unaccounted cupboards or doors. Keep in mind that we are looking into the possibility that there is a way that patients could have been treated or housed here away from the eyes of others."

"Like prisons?"

"I have no idea SJ. I don't want you mentioning any of this outside of our team. Not to your mothers or friends or anyone, under pain of disciplinary action."

"OK boss. We are only joking around, it's pretty scary in here and I'm trying to keep the mood light."

"I understand," acknowledged Revie. "I've been in here before and can guarantee that there are lots of noises and shadows that will distract you. I doubt very much that they are ghosts. Keep your torches on and stick together. This is an old building and although it looks tidy, there could be hazards about. I don't want any accidents."

"Use your radios if you must, but phones will be easier. Everyone got our numbers? Brake? You go with the Jones pair, keep an eye on them and on everything else." said Buchanan.

They all affirmed and the three set off down the corridor until they reached the oak staircase and ran up it. Revie and Buchanan heard chattering as they went, but sight and sound were soon lost. The two senior officers stood together quietly.

"Fuck, it's gone cold," said Buchanan. "It's like someone just opened a freezer door."

"Probably a draught," said Revie.

"Why don't they have the power connected?"

"That caretaker told me it's because of intruders, they don't want to encourage them. I expect the bills were big here when it was running though."

"I don't doubt it. You know, I can't work out whether we are looking for something that isn't there or being thorough detectives," mused Buchanan.

"We have to cover all angles, because there have been precious few leads so far. We've got lots of speculation, but nothing to hang my hat on. Four bodies who no one can identify, ghostly goings on and a bunch of missing people. You think something would turn up."

"I have only found out facts and figures on that case I told you about, The Red Gable one. There are links to Tresaith and this place, but it's almost a conspiracy theory and I'm not used to that."

A door slammed in front of the two officers and they both jumped.

"Fuck, fuck, fuck," said Revie. "I'm getting jumpier the more often I come in here."

"It will just be the wind," said Buchanan, more hopefully than he cared to admit.

"Maybe, but who would that nurse be walking away from us?"

"Jesus H… Hey miss! We are police officers. Can you help us?" The nurse turned around, very slowly and the temperature dropped several degrees again. Their breath smoked in front of their faces. She stood facing them, standing 3 metres in front, but said nothing.

"We didn't expect to see anyone here tonight. What are you doing here?"

"Are you from the future or the past?" she asked.

The men looked at each other, "It's August 2005, if that helps," Revie informed her.

"What would help, is you turning off your torches. I am almost blind. I work here and am in the middle of seeing the patients who are going to bed. This is a very busy time of the day and visiting times are over. Off you go." She wheeled around and walked through a doorway to the left.

Buchanan took off after her and followed her through the swing doors and into the ward. He was surprised to note that the ward was laid out as he would have expected if it were in use. Pulling his attention back to the job in hand, he followed the nurse through a door at the back of the ward and into another corridor. She got into a lift and the door closed and he heard the whirring of the cables as it went down. He bashed the lift button as he looked around. His head torch had slipped down slightly and he adjusted it with his free hand. Scanning the corridor, he noticed the nurse standing at the end of the corridor smiling at him. Leaving the lift, he ran after her as she trotted down some stairs. Down and down she went and Buchanan followed her. He felt very light headed by the time he reached the bottom. The base of the stairs ended in a small lobby with three oak doors leading off. He saw the nurse go through one and the door swinging to and fro. As it opened briefly before closing again, Buchanan saw a dimly lit corridor along which the nurse ran. He did not feel that he could follow, the ice cold breeze had returned and he was suddenly painfully aware that he was a long way from his colleagues. No one had followed and he did not think that they would know where he was because he had left so suddenly. Come to think of it, he didn't know where he was. He had followed a ghost nurse and not paid attention to where he was going.

He raised and lowered his shoulders in an exaggerated fashion as he took several deep breaths. There was a rising anxiety within him, he had suffered badly from agoraphobia several years ago and he had been almost debilitated during his university years. It had cost him a degree at Oxford and he still mourned it. He had eventually cured himself after meeting a Buddhist monk and practicing mindfulness. But now, he recognised the shivering signs of its return at the edges of his mind. If he allowed it to resurface while he was in the dark, on his own, in a deserted asylum, he would be in more trouble than he could imagine...

His head torch went out and the dark was as dark as it could be. He tried to listen for his colleagues, but could hear nothing so he sat down on the floor. He wanted to shout for help, but what if that caused…? Caused what? He got up and tried to open the doors leading off from the lobby, but that occupation left him breathless and panicky. He was sweating and frightened, worse when none of the doors would open. His radio and his phone! How could he be so fucking stupid? He searched his pockets and found the radio. It was dead. His phone was dead too and he had an alarming recollection that being in the presence of spirits would drain batteries. He must go back upstairs and try and retrace his steps.

He knew he hadn't turned right nor left since following the nurse down the stairs from the lift shaft. If he could only get back there he could shout for his colleagues, they were bound to be looking for him. Why couldn't he shout for them now? He could hardly breathe while his mind was busy reminding him of panic. He tried to control his panic and didn't have time for logical thoughts.   He had been in this state before, stranded in the middle of Broad Street, Oxford and not being able to remember which college he studied at. Students had looked at him and giggled and some made rude comments and pushed him around. Later he realised that hadn't actually happened, he had become rigid in mind and body during his panic. But no one had noticed at all, he had added the insults as a memory trimming. He had no friends and no enemies at Oxford and no one noticed when he left.

Ever since that time, he had lost himself in study and single minded concentration on whatever job he decided to do.

He reached out and found the banister and began to walk up. He went slowly because he was so breathless from his panic. It was as though his chest was shrinking and he knew that he must wait until the relaxation arrived and freed his breath. He should wait before he moved, but did not want to remain in Ghostville at the stair bottom.

It wasn't getting any fucking lighter as he climbed up, and it wasn't getting any easier to breathe. The feeling of being kicked in the chest by a horse was suffocating. He had suffered in this way when the attacks were upon him years ago and now he recognised the return of these symptoms and he feared for his immediate future. He dragged himself up the banister until he thought about the ghosts he dreaded and how they might try and touch him and so he removed his hands.

Now, DS Colin Buchanan was crawling on his hands and knees up unknown dirty stairs in an effort to save his life. As he fell into a faint, he was vaguely aware of faces looking concerned about him. There was light and a strange smell – his colleagues must be here.

PART THREE

CHAPTER FOURTEEN

Colin was aware of a large light in front of him similar to the floodlights at a rugby match.

"Where am I?" he thought he said out loud. But he couldn't hear any noise outside his head.

The light was really bright and it wasn't a floodlight. It was one of those you see over a bed in an operating theatre. Perhaps he had been taken to Bodelwyddan and was going to have an operation. A man wearing a surgical mask and a cap leant over him and said,

"I think he's still conscious nurse. Give him a bit more."

"Yes sir," answered the small woman, similarly attired.

"Make sure I'm out of it before you stick any knives in me," Colin said again - silently.

"Scalpel, nurse. No that's not a scalpel you stupid twat, that's some sort of surgical thingy."

"I think he can still hear us sir. Look his eyes are darting really quickly from side to side. Look."

The surgeon looked and appeared unhappy with what he saw.

"Pass that hammer. We need to hit him on the head."

Colin was vaguely aware of a commotion and breaking glass and shouts of, "Dr. Tresaith! I was trying to help, we found him like that and he was dying!"

A woman's voice followed,

"Sir, I don't know how you got in here, but I am Dr. Tresaith and I will look after you now. Do not worry about what just happened, I will explain it all when you are feeling better."

She turned away and said to someone out of view, "Check his vitals for me Joseph."

"They are fine Doctor, his heart is just beating a bit irregular."

"That's good, excellent. You just go back to sleep now and when you wake up, all will be well."

Colin closed his eyes guessing he was probably dreaming anyway.

*

When he woke again, he was feeling much better. He had a slight flash of belief that he had awoken in his own bed following a bad dream, but that thought left him really quickly. Through slit eyes obscured by a blinding headache, he looked carefully around the room he was laying in.

This was a dark room, apparently lit by bulbs which gave out the dimmed down brown light, common during the 1940's. Perhaps he was dreaming still.

There was a screen alongside him made from cream silk which was attached to a metal frame. He hadn't seen one like that since – probably ever. His bed had a pale green bedspread over a white sheet and at the end of his bed was a foot rail upon which hung a metal clipboard. He moved his head slightly to the right and noticed a cabinet upon which stood a jug and a glass.

He tried to shout out,

"Hello! Is there anyone around?"

He was unsure how loudly he had spoken and whether those words had only been in his head. His hearing appeared to be working however, as he heard the quick light footsteps of a nurse who was soon by his side.

"Feeling better are we Mr Buchanan? You have had a nasty time, but everything is fine now."

She took his wrist and held it while she checked her breast watch which she held up in order to see the clock face at its correct orientation.

"That's all as it should be," she announced and placed his wrist back onto the bed.

"Where am I?" he asked.

"You are in hospital Mr Buchanan, at Tresaith."

"Tresaith? I need to speak to my boss. I need my phone."

"All those who need to know have been told. They will visit you as soon as you are well enough but you have to rest now." The nurse held up a syringe from which she sent a small shower of liquid into the air. She brought it down to his arm and injected. Colin was aware of a slight sting and a darkening of his awareness.

It was the laughter which woke him up. It was the sound of a mad woman and was swiftly followed by shouts of,

"Betty, Betty, do be quiet! Go back to your room immediately."

"I shall take her Dr. Tresaith," said another woman.

Colin realised that he was moaning and was suddenly comforted by the feeling of a warm hand upon his forehead.

"Don't worry Mr Buchanan. In spite of all evidence to the contrary and I am well aware that you have a great interest in evidence, you are safe here in this room. But, please mind that you do not leave this room without supervision. The hospital itself is not particularly safe. Now, ssshhh."

"I am not tired Doctor I want to speak to my boss, can you please get me my phone and my things."

"Your phone won't do you any good Mr Buchanan and I don't currently have access to your things."

Colin tried to raise himself from the bed, but felt incredibly weak.

"You see, you are not quite ready to sit up yet. Don't panic about the strange sensations you are experiencing. It is just your condition and will soon pass."

Dr Tresaith smiled at her patient and left the room. This time Colin did not go back to sleep, although he did close his eyes as she walked out of the room. He tried again to sit up and although he succeeded, the room spun so violently that he was put in mind of being drunk during his teen years. He brought in his meditation training and breathed calmly and deeply until the spinning stopped.

Now he could get a better comprehension of his problem. The room he was in had no outside windows and very little furniture. He had a sense of being back in time as he noted the room contents and basic medical equipment sitting on the small table in the far corner. As he removed the cover and swung his legs out of the bed, his feet met the cold floor and he searched in vain for some sort of shoe or slipper there. He found neither and instead staggered over to a cupboard. He wanted his clothes to cover the embarrassment that was currently in the style of his entire back side being visible to the elements.

He soon discovered that there was nothing secreted in the drawers and no gown hanging on the back of the door. He was feeling cold and weak and a little frightened now. He tried the door and discovered it locked and resisting his efforts. He banged on the door and shouted for help. A voice the other side said,

"They won't come and help you, you know. Now you are here, you are never going home. None of us are going home."

This announcement was followed by a thud and a squeak and silence. Colin was feeling scared but thankfully not panicked and he could cope with fear. He was no coward.

Colin went back to his bed and sat upon it. He poured and drank some of the water and felt a little calmer. He then took the cover from his bed and wrapped around his body, toga style. He picked up two pieces of wire from the table and straightened them out. He set about picking the lock on the door, a skill learnt during his police career. He was patient and soon successful in his task and as the door opened he carefully looked outside. The corridor was lit in a similar fashion to his room with subdued bulbs burning as if in a brown out.

He could see no person in the green and cream tiled corridor and the doors which were visible to him all appeared to be closed. He adjusted his toga and carefully walked off to his left. After almost of a minute of travel he noticed a door over which was a sign informing him that the Medical Superintendent should be in residence.

He tried the door and discovered that it was open. If there was someone there, he was prepared to insist on speaking to Revie and use his most authoritative tone.

He had a feeling that it was night-time, but the lack of windows and dimmed lighting may have been giving him that impression.

He pushed open the door and found the room in complete darkness. Using the dim light coming from the corridor he eventually found a table lamp and switched it on. All the while he felt the sensation of freezing rain about his body and was unnerved as if he was being haunted. He looked for a telephone and found one hidden under a doctor's gown at the edge of the desk. He listened for the dialling tone and then pushed the buttons, dialling 999 as without his own phone he could not recall Revie's actual number.

He felt relief at hearing the ring tone and waited for it to be answered. Sadly he waited in vain and the line continued to ring out. Colin returned the phone to its cradle and began looking around the office. From the papers and documents he discovered there, he could only deduce that he must be in one of the old offices no longer used. He did find some men's clothes in a cupboard and although he felt an initial queasiness at putting on another man's trousers, this he overcame and swiftly dressed.

The trainers were a size too large for him, but absolutely better than nothing. His giddiness had left him but he still felt weak and assumed this would remain with him until he had some food and a proper rest. There was no chance of that for the moment and so he left the room much happier now that his arse was safely hidden under a clean pair of jeans and a Leeds United sweatshirt.

The corridor was still quiet but he strode out with more confidence than before and pushed through the swing doors separating this part of the corridor from the next. He continued for two minutes before he heard voices in one of the rooms to his right. This room had a wide open door which revealed a group of women holding down another woman on the bed. He was about to demand their attention as a police officer might when he was held from behind by two men. One of the women in the room came out and said,

"Let him go, let him go."

"I demand that you let me speak to my office, Dr. Tresaith. This is criminal!"

"Come along to my office Mr Buchanan. Judging by your outfit, I see you have been there already. Jonny take over from me, Linda needs help to calm down. Come on, walk with me."

Colin walked with the doctor and was glad of it as he was feeling weak again and was trying not to faint.

"I expect you are still feeling weak, Mr Buchanan. You probably need some food."

"How long have I been here?"

"A week, you have been here a week since my staff found you on one of the landings. Come on in here."

She beckoned to the chair he had recently left his toga hanging from. She laughed when she found it and said,

"Ingenious. I shall remember that next time."

Dr. Tresaith pressed a buzzer and a voice crackled through,

"Yes Dr?"

"Coffee and sandwiches to my office please. And cake, for two." Dr Tresaith looked at Colin and asked, "Ham, cheese or beef? Oh and apparently we still have salad."

"Beef salad please," he answered. He was starving.

Dr. Tresaith relayed the order and said,

"I can't let you speak to your boss, or leave here for that matter."

Colin quelled the panic, he would be better with food.

"You cannot prevent it, unless, of course, you want to be arrested."

Dr. Tresaith laughed.

"I am not trying to prevent you Mr Buchanan. I would dearly love to leave this place with you but I can't speak to anyone outside either."

They were disturbed by a man whom, Colin vaguely recognised, wheeling a trolley containing plates of sandwiches, cakes and coffee. He had the brightest beam upon his scarred face and presented the feast with genuine pride.

"Thanks Darren. We are very grateful." The man nodded and left the room.

"Darren is one of our great successes. He has been with us for years."

"I see, or rather I don't see. Explain to me why neither of us is able to leave this – wherever we are."

"Eat some food Mr Buchanan. And I will give you a brief resume of our predicament."

CHAPTER FIFTEEN

Selina Tresaith told Colin about the hidden patients and the money the family received to keep them out of the public eye. She told him of the involvement of Dr. Wright and various members of staff whom Buchanan had already interviewed. When she told him about the transfer of official patients to other hospitals and the conundrum about the secret wards, Colin began to understand what had happened.

"So we gradually trained some of the more established and trustworthy patients to care for the hidden residents and when upstairs finally closed, none of them went upstairs again. The family had already built this massive, underground network years ago and so once we added the extra medical supplies and food, we knew that we would be safe here for a while."

"And since then your family has been involved in the maintenance of down here?"

"Yes they have and Dr. Wright has too. I thought he and I would get together officially but he reversed away from me and decided to run off to Canada. He is an absolute bastard."

"He is involved too then. All these people out and out lied to us."

"Of course they did, they were hardly likely to confess. This a big deal with potential prison time if we are ever found out. But, no one is ever going to discover us down here."

"I did and they will be looking for me."

"They will be looking for you but they won't find you. You didn't find anything did you? And your Inspector Revie hasn't found anything in three visits."

"I saw a ghost in the old hospital, I just remembered that."

"Ha. Those ghosts are some of our residents. I told you that no one ever dies down here, they just go to sleep and wake up in the same state. We all do, we only notice when other people die and don't notice when we die. We just carry on doing and imagining the same rubbish. But that discussion is for a different day. Anyway, the real old ones are able to imagine themselves upstairs and around the grounds of the Asylum. They don't travel beyond the perimeter you know - not past those old stone walls."

"So why don't you do that?" Yea, Colin could now see that he was still in a dream.

"I'm not old enough or sick enough and I am aware of the process. I need to stay in my body in order to look after the other patients. If I don't, they will starve and die horribly. I couldn't have that on my conscience."

"Naturally," he answered. "And what about those four bodies in the mortuary? Were they down to you?"

"Bodies? Christ, is that where they ended up? That's something else I need to tell you. If our patients go walkabout upstairs or spookabout I should say and don't make it back in time. Well, they sort of solidify and can't breathe and then die. My family usually get rid of them in the old furnaces but something stopped them this time. My brother John is pretty good with the old mortician skills."

"You still speak to your family?"

"Not by any means you would recognise," she answered. "Not these days anyway. We used to have much more communication but somehow the gates closed and we couldn't leave here and they couldn't come down. I was hoping that by you arriving here, you could let me know how you did it."

Colin looked at her and answered, "Assuming that I am not dreaming still and I'm not sure about that at all, I can easily tell you. I had a panic attack chasing a fucking ghost and then got lost and then passed out and woke up in that ward."

"You can't remember anything that happened in between?"

"Some faces and an operating theatre."

"Oh yeah, I'm sorry about that."

"And the rest you know. They will be looking for me, the rest of the team."

"They will be looking I agree. Don't worry about your memory, it will come back. And when it does, we can all get out of this fucking place."

CHAPTER SIXTEEN

Colin was waiting to wake up. The trouble was, as far as he could recollect he had been in the old Asylum for about a month and he hadn't woken up yet, nor had anyone come to look for him.

So he was either delusional – or this was real.

"Colin!" Everyone used his first name. He hadn't heard DS Buchanan for a while now and he had lost his feeling of authority over anyone. Selina Tresaith had told him that unless something else was to occur, he was stuck there along with the rest of them and so he may as well start working for his keep.

He was medic trained, partly because of his job and partly because he renewed his qualifications every three years in order to maintain his Mountain Leader status. He used these skills to assist with the patients although he was learning that there was little call for trauma medicine. There were mild illnesses such as colds and stomach upsets and some minor wound dressings. No one ever really got ill and no one was damaged physically and so there was little for him to do.

The mental problems were mainly anxiety, depression and OCD. Horrible for the sufferer but treatable and certainly none of those diagnoses would incarcerate a person these days.

There were however, some patients who needed locking away permanently and Roy Townsend was one of these patients. His wife still pootled about the place in a wheelchair, believing that she was on holiday with Roy for a couple of weeks. Roy was locked in his room and staff only went in two at a time, it was too dangerous to do anything else. Roy knew where he was and why he was there and he would often try and get some of the other patients on his side. Many patients thought he was a good man who had influence with the high ups and was therefore an ally they needed.

This was where Colin's police duties came to the fore. He was assigned to watching what Townsend and a few other names were up to. On one of their regular meetings in her office, Dr. Tresaith had said that they were to keep on top of their game.

"They are always planning an escape and when they discover that they cannot leave, sometimes they take it out on one of the other residents. And there is always the chance that they will find a way out."

"I keep looking for that way out myself," said Colin.

"I spent years doing that on and off and I was brought up with knowledge of the place. I have wondered whether we are in some sort of parallel universe down here."

"Or just dead."

"I've wondered that too. My thoughts get very complicated and confused the longer we have been lost."

"But if we are dead, there must still be a way out. It can't be like this forever."

"You'd hope not, wouldn't you?"

They left the office together and walked towards Roy Townsend's room. Colin had agreed to accompany Selina on this visit.

Roy was lying down on his bed, eyes closed and hands behind his head. He did not move nor open his eyes when they entered his space.

He spoke, "To what do I owe this pleasure? Is the law trying to catch up with me finally?"

"Does the law need to catch up with you Mr Townsend?"

"I have no idea son. I've been down here that long now I could have reincarnated into another body. So you tell me."

"That's not likely to have happened is it?" said Dr. Tresaith.

"Reincarnation and rebirth have been happening to quite a lot of patients here, as you well know Dr. Tresaith."

"I'm not so sure that is true," she answered.

"So how exactly are you accounting for the travelling patients and the missing ones? How do you explain no one being able to leave or get in here? That hasn't happened for years. Unless we count you copper. You've probably died like the rest of us have."

Roy Townsend opened his eyes.

"And another fucking thing, Doctor. I've heard that we are going to be running out of food and medicine any day now. What do you intend to do about that?"

Selina Tresaith ignored her patient and held out her hand.

"I need to take your blood pressure Mr Townsend. It's been too high recently and we need to keep on top of it. We don't want you dropping dead of a stroke or heart attack, do we?"

Roy appeared a little chastened Colin thought and he sat up in bed and removed his jacket. Selina took his blood pressure, shaking her head as she did so. Colin didn't think that this type of bedside manner was going to instil calm in her patient, knowing that if his doctor spoke and acted as she, he would have assumed he was going to have an imminent seizure. This bedside talk was in direct conflict to her prior instructions and he assumed that Selina wanted Roy to die.

"You have got to calm down, Mr Townsend. Stop winding yourself up so much. I've heard about you upsetting everyone else again, so stop it."

"I'm not calming down until you let me leave this nuthouse." He rolled down his shirt sleeve and returned his jacket to his back.

"None of us appear to be leaving this nuthouse," answered Selina as she beckoned Colin to follow her out. Colin took a last look around the room which housed nothing more than the cells back at the station did. Only this cell was a damn sight colder and darker than back at the nick.

Colin missed home and his job and his friends, although technically he didn't really have any friends because he worked all the time. His colleagues didn't appreciate his efforts a belief proved by the fact that he was transferred from department to department so regularly and none of his colleagues ever rang to see how he was doing. His family - he didn't like to think about his family. Perhaps no one was looking for him.

He was happy that he did not have a wife and child to worry about him.

"Is he right about the food and medicine situation?" he asked as they stepped back into the corridor.

"It is true that we are running low on supplies. We had a huge stock of everything in case there was ever an emergency but to be honest stock is thinning out quicker than I would like. We need to find a way out of here."

"And you have checked everywhere?"

"Of course and as I said, staff and patients have been secretly trying to do it for years. I would know if there was a way."

"What's this about parallel universes and spirit travel? I know it's crazy but it must be based on something?"

"It isn't crazy. The ones who do leave, temporarily or permanently, do so with their minds and not with their bodies."

"Ok."

"You should have a talk with Joseph, he will explain better than I can. But you have to wait until he is in the right frame of mind and that is a rare phenomenon these days."

Selina walked in front of him and he naturally followed.

CHAPTER SEVENTEEN

Selina turned and bowed in front of Joseph's room and outstretched her arm to shown Colin the way in. Even though he had been in Joseph's room several times already, he bowed in response and they both laughed as he knocked on the door. As he turned round, he noticed she had gone and for a fleeting moment he was sorry.

Joseph answered almost immediately.

"Hello Mr Scottish Policeman, come into my parlour and sit with me. I have had tea brought in so that we will not be disturbed while we speak."

Colin sat on the chair he was beckoned to and accepted the proffered cup. He chose some sandwiches from the china stand and placed them on his plate.

"You remind me of Superintendent Colin Watson," said Joseph.

"Oh. Which police force?"

"No police force. He used to be the Medical Superintendent here years ago. He was a nice man and very kind to me. He arranged dances and parties for us all. He left and went back to Edinburgh and never came back."

"I had a grandfather called Colin Watson but I don't see how it could have been the same man."

"Why not?"

Colin didn't know why not. He hadn't known his maternal grandfather but it would have been more than miraculous for them both to be involved with Tresaith Asylum.

"I don't know. When I get out of here, I will find out."

"Is he still alive?"

"No, I don't think so. He might be but he would be really old now. I don't have anything to do with that side of my family."

"I never had anything to do with my family either. It's a bit difficult to be a loving person when you don't feel loved isn't it?"

"It is, Joseph. I was wondering if you knew a way I can leave here? Dr. Tresaith intimated that there is a way?"

"Oh, she has decided to let you in on that secret has she?"

"I don't know. She just said that I should speak to you."

"It must be an emergency – or she likes you."

"All I know is that there could be a problem looming large if I don't find my way out."

"Because your colleagues will be worried about you?"

"I doubt they will be worried about me. They were probably more worried about their own careers when they lost me."

"That is so sad. I have my own sad story which I do not dwell upon. My family were not quite as helpful as they might have been. But that is the story of many in here and we don't miss them really."

"I have been told about your story and many of the others," answered Colin.

"Well, don't worry about yourself Colin. There is still time for you to have a great life. Now tell me more about your problems."

"They are not mine, they are everyone's problems. It seems that we are quickly running out of food and medicine. There is no way out that has yet been found and we need to find one."

"That is easy and difficult. You need to think yourself out of here and then for a while you will travel and people will only perceive you as a ghost. If you continue, you will eventually materialise where you want to be."

"That's very interesting but I am not a believer in that sort of junk."

"Ha-ha! You will be eventually, Mr Buchanan. Perhaps for now we need to get into the secondary vault and open that. It's full of food, medicine, clothes and all the paraphernalia we need. It was your grandfather who suggested that the asylum should have a back-up store."

"There is another vault? Dr Tresaith doesn't seem to know about it."

"Well she wouldn't. Her brother sorted it out. I believe he arranged all the stock himself and that way he was paid a huge amount from the business that the rest of his family did not have a share in."

"I suppose if we can get in there, it will have been worth the money he earned."

"Yes. Shall I show you where I think it is? We will need a couple of the old rezzies to help us out with this."

Joseph swung his legs off his bed and walked towards his door,

"Come on Mr Buchanan. Let's see what we can find."

Colin followed his new friend out into the corridor. He noticed how much of a swing in his step Joseph had now. He was happily in charge.

"Are we going to speak to Dr. Tresaith first, do you think?"

"No, we shouldn't get her hopes up Joseph. We might not be able to find the store."

Joseph laughed as he turned suddenly through a doorway and ran swiftly down the stairs there. Colin hadn't noticed this door before. Perhaps he just hadn't been shown it.

Joseph arrived at another door and knocked with some sort of special knock, which Colin tried to remember, not having expected it. Was it knock, tap, tap, tap? That was it, Colin thought. The door opened swiftly and Colin noticed two men he did not think he had seen before.

"Mr Buchanan, this is Jonny Stone and George Smith. Guys, Mr Buchanan is a Scottish policeman who has gone and got himself stuck here at our home."

The men nodded, smiled and reached out with their hands. Colin shook each hand in return and appreciated their friendliness.

"Jonny and George have been here since 1917, is that right?"

"We were sent here because we were going to be sent back to the Front and we were both suffering very badly with our nerves," said Jonny.

"Is called PTSD these days but back then they shot you," informed George.

"They did," agreed Colin. "Thank goodness times have changed."

"We are still stuck in an Asylum though," said George sadly.

Colin couldn't think of a polite way to answer that. Instead, he said,

"Joseph tells me that you know where there is another store? It seems to main stores are running low and as we don't appear to be getting out of here anytime soon, we need to get hold of the stocks."

The men looked at each other and pulled faces.

"We have a pretty good idea where but we haven't actually been there," said Jonny.

"We knew they were building and stocking another place but they kept us all on lockdown while they were doing it. We sort of worked out with our engineering abilities where it could possibly be." George was opening a diagram as he explained. This he rolled out on to the table around which they all sat.

"We will have to get into the main building on the ground floor and then go down stairs again under the cells," said Joseph.

"I thought the whole point was that we can't leave the building," interrupted Colin.

"That's only true in a manner of speaking. We can leave but we can't be seen and we can't let go of where we are down here. It's a complicated arrangement," said George.

"And one I do not understand," Colin grinned.

"The only way to understand is to come and see." The three men, animated now with the mission held the door open for him and ushered him through.

They moved quickly along the corridor, which Colin surmised must be two floors lower than the floor he had been living on these past months. How many floors this was beneath the actual asylum he felt was about to be revealed to him.

Jonny stopped by the wall facing them and slapped it.

"It's behind there," he announced.

"So we knock through?" asked Colin.

"Not a chance. No. We have to go up and over. That's what we have to do."

CHAPTER EIGHTEEN

Going up three flights of steps was easy enough, Colin decided. He had kept a modicum of fitness during his incarceration and he was pleased for that. He reached the top landing several minutes before his new friends and was incredibly pleased with himself. Then he realised how old his mates were and stopped inwardly grinning.

Joseph, Jonny and George were chattering with each other as they reached the landing and Jonny said,

"We have just been talking about the next step. If you hadn't been sprinting ahead of us, we wouldn't have to repeat ourselves now."

Colin nodded. He had no intention of keeping to their speed and be on a fast track to old age or madness.

"What's next?" he asked.

You see that door there? We go through there and we will be in the asylum itself. But... you must remember that it will seem as though you are back. This is not true. No one can see you properly, you will be as a ghost."

"I still don't understand what is going on here."

"You are going to see life as it really is. Everyone's life is a result of their imagination and they will only get what they believe. It's that simple and virtually no one understands it. Life is like a dream – it is a dream and everyone's believes everyone else's dream without realising it is a dream."

"Right - now I understand it," said Colin in mock appreciation.

"Come on then."

They pushed open the door and the sensations of his last visit to the floor of the deserted asylum washed over him. It was the damp, the dust and the cold, only now there was something else.

They were standing in the corridor which Colin remembered led to wards and one of the halls. The walls were covered in graffiti and there was smashed glass in the windows and doors.

"What the hell has happened here?" he asked.

"This is what happens when people begin to believe that ghosts and demons have occupied the place. Then the idea attracts vandals, druggies, people who want sex in a strange place and fanatics. What most of them want to do is smash the place up for some reason," said George.

"We know why they do it. The vandals that is, they have issues of some sort or another and the patients hang on to them and egg them on," answered Jonny.

"The patients? From downstairs?" asked Colin.

"Oh yes. There are still a lot of patients with demons of their own and they get a lot of pleasure from attaching themselves to people who deserve it," explained Joseph.

"And some of the patients are hoping to get a free trip out of here. They think that if they stay close to the vandals, then they will be able to follow them home," said Jonny.

"Some of them have got a long way though. I mean even further that the boundaries and we aren't supposed to be getting beyond the boundary wall," pointed out Jonny.

"Well there is also supposed to be a tunnel link to the house and we haven't found that yet either," said George.

"I always thought that Dr. Tresaith must know about it. She can't have been involved her entire life and not know about another way out. It's just that she never tells us."

"Perhaps she likes it here Joseph. Perhaps it's the only place she feels comfortable."

Colin listened with interest but did not join in on the conversation. He still found it difficult to believe that Selina did not know how to leave the asylum. He assumed that she was frightened of the criminal action she would face once she left. And if she was bothered by that, then there was no way that she was going to allow Detective Sergeant Buchanan to leave alive.

Colin walked into the corridor and made his way directly to the smashed doorway. He walked through and turned back. His fellow escapees looked at him and smiled. They clearly did not think that he was going to be getting out. He stopped to check around the yard which he seemed to remember had been where patients were once allowed to walk in the fresh air. Now it was littered with bricks and defaced boarding which had previously been nailed up at the windows. He walked and scrunched his way to the far end of the quad and looked back at the main building he had just left. This was equally battered by weather and he saw plants growing from the ground which had wound their way up the building walls. The clock tower at the top looked as though it had been shot at and he saw a rat scurrying along the edge of the wall.

"How long have I been down there?" Colin said out loud.

"Longer than you think," answered Joseph.

Colin shrugged off Joseph's arm from his shoulder and ran towards the driveway which circumnavigated the hospital. He followed it round to the front of the asylum and stopped again. From here he could see the grand gothic front of the asylum, now chipped and spoilt by paint graffiti. The main oak doors were covered in thick boarding which was emblazoned with the words.

KEEP OUT – DANGER

daubed across it in red.

Colin ignored the shouts of the others and he ran the 250 metres towards the closed main gates and rattled them. He was breathless and panicky. He saw no cars or people on the road out front but he shouted anyway. Jonny caught up with him,

"I told you that you can't escape. It's like it's not real. If you stood here all day screaming and shouting, no one would come. Don't you think we've tried? All we seem able to do is attach ourselves to those who break in. I told you this already."

"It's fucking stupid," answered Colin.

"Well that's as maybe, as I seem to remember my grandma saying," said George, endeavouring to lighten the mood.

"But it's not going to help us find this store is it?" added Joseph.

They had all followed him.

"I will help you find the store," said Colin. "But then I'm coming straight back here and finding a way out."

"I'll help you with that if you want me too," said Jonny. "But I am advising you not to tell Dr. Tresaith."

"There are also a few others he shouldn't tell," agreed George.

"Sadly, not everyone is trustworthy," added Joseph.

Colin took them at their word but was determined to get himself out of Tresaith Asylum somehow.

"Come on. We don't want to be out after dark," Joseph reminded them.

There was urgency about the men and Colin caught the mood and followed them back around the driveway. They soon reached a second quadrangle surrounded by small buildings, which Colin remembered had housed the tailors shop, cobblers and upholsterers back in the day. Jonny ran into the cobbler's shop and by the time everyone else reached them, he was pulling back the bench and opening a trapdoor.

"Here we are," he announced as he revealed a set of stairs.

"Have you been down there before?" asked Colin, feeling a little anxious again.

"Yes. It's quite safe, so don't worry," said Jonny.

He scurried down the steps, while his companions remained at the surface.

"I'm doing this on my own," he shouted back and the others followed him down.

It was dark, very dark going down and Colin used his well-rehearsed technique which generally prevented the onset of his claustrophobia. He had imagined that living below ground for the past – however long it was – would cure him of his panics. But he recognised the shortness of breath and slowed his pace.

Joseph said, "We all feel a bit weird Colin, it's not just you."

Colin smiled, he was grateful for the kindness shown. He felt a little guilty when he remembered that he had always been judgmental in regard to people with mental health issues and yet here he was being shown understanding and given comfort. It would have been nice if his family and supposed friends had ever done the same. He slowly followed Joseph down.

Jonny shouted up, "There are a couple of lanterns here men. Who has got a match?"

George proffered a box and soon the lanterns were lit and the corridor appeared in semi darkness .To the left of the stairs the corridor scampered into an unknown distance. To the right was two metres of tiled floor, ending with a double door.

"This is our way out people." He drew the bolts and unlocked the locks using the large key sitting in the keyhole. As he pulled the doors, he revealed the corridor from their side of the hospital.

"That means that the stores are along this corridor somewhere," said Colin. Should he take charge? He was a copper.

"It is," agreed Jonny. "We should close this access point first though."

"The cobbler's?" asked Colin.

"Yea, would you mind doing that? I think it would be best if only a few of us know about this place."

Colin nodded and ran up the stairs. He was glad of the excuse to get out into the air again. He climbed back into the workshop and went over to the door. Before he went to lock it, he opened it and looked outside. Marching purposefully across the quadrangle and away from him was a group of young people. He guessed that they were probably in their twenties. They had rucksacks and weatherproof coats and hats. They laughed and joked and pushed each other around. Instinctively he shouted to them. Only one turned round and looked in their direction.

"Ssshhh you lot. Did you hear that? Did you hear someone shouting?"

"No you fucktard. This bit won't be haunted, will it?"

"Why not? The other parts are. Why wouldn't this part be?"

Colin picked up some stones and walked towards the now stationary group. He threw them all in their direction. Apparently that action was visible and the group squealed and jumped and scattered.

"Fuckety, fuck, fuck. You must have heard that!"

"Look, there are stones on the ground." He picked them up. "See, they are hot!"

The stones were passed around the group who all agreed that, yes, the stones were hot.

"We should get some good results tonight," announced one who was now holding a camera, redeemed from his rucksack.

"There's nothing around now."

Colin shouted loudly into the ear of the camera guy and tugged on his arm. The man turned round sharply and Colin saw that the camera was pointing directly at him. He shouted into it,

"If one of you can hear me, I'm Detective Sergeant Colin Buchanan and I am stuck here somehow. Speak to DI Revie and tell him to look underneath the asylum. He will find me there. Help me. Help me."

"Oy!"

Colin swung round and saw Jonny beckoning him back.

"Don't bother with those stupid buggers. They will never hear you."

"They seemed to hear something," he answered.

"They hear what they want. And before you start to get all romantic about them, remember that they are the bastards who have been systematically wrecking the place over the years. Those lot and loads like them."

He led Colin back to the cobbler's shop and as they locked the door behind them, Colin watched the group. He thought that the camera man was following them with his lens, but he may have been mistaken.

CHAPTER NINETEEN

"Do these people see us?" Colin asked Jonny.

"I think some of them do, most don't. Some of the other rezzies are sure that they are communicating with the trespassers. That's what they are doing, trespassing. They are intent on damage and disruption and they film and record what they think they see. They take drugs and have sex and bully the caretaker and in the main are a bunch of twats."

"Right, do the police ever come here?"

"You mean your mates? I believe they looked for a while, but they haven't been back here for years. I don't think they are looking for you now if that's what you are wondering."

"No, I wasn't really."

"Liar," said Jonny.

"I can't work out what's going on at all. The time thing and the fact I can't leave here. I'm pretty sure I'm dreaming or dead, although I suspect that the two states are the same."

"Yes, the whole thing is a dream. Ooooooooo!"

Colin ignored the comment and went down the steps and Jonny shut the trapdoor behind them. The others were waiting for them.

"We started down the corridor once already but you guys took too long to join us," said George.

"Did you find the storeroom?" asked Jonny.

Joseph replied, "We found some massive doors and a couple of other corridors, but we didn't go down either of those in case we got lost and the lantern went out."

"And we didn't try and open the doors without all of us being there. There might be something spooky in there," added George.

Opening the double doors was easy, there wasn't even a lock. It was the smell that they all noticed first - sweet and savoury, rubber and dust and above all decay.

"There's a lot of stuff in here," noted George.

"We will have to check everything before we use it. Some of this stuff could be poisonous," said Colin, reverting again to his police role.

"We should get more people here to take an inventory and go thought the stock."

"But George, we don't trust most of the others. So let's think carefully before we tell anyone."

"Who don't you trust?" asked Colin.

"It's a long list," said Jonny. "Townsend and Parry, they will try and make profit and gain power. Dr.

Tresaith, she will want to keep some fear going or she will have a riot on her hands."

"Once they get wind that supplies are low, there will be a messy riot anyway," added George.

"True and there are some others in the hospital who keep themselves to themselves and won't get involved with any group."

"It looks as though there are plenty of medical supplies and food and drink," said Colin.

"There is plenty of linen and some clothes. We have to keep control of all this you know. It will be a free for all if we let the others in," said Jonny, turning over a huge box of soap powder.

Colin stood back from the group because he was remembering that this storeroom was supposed to be accessed from the manor. He had to check that out – but should he tell the others? He decided against it, perhaps it would be better if they thought that he had had another panic attack.

Colin quietly left the storeroom, and turned right at the door. He had taken a couple of torches he had found on a shelf and several packs of batteries. Some potentially out of date energy drinks and a box of energy bars completed his haul. He didn't want to be left without if he got trapped or something equally horrific. He also didn't want to turn on the torches until he was sure that the back shadow from it would not attract attention from his companions. He wanted to get out of this place and preferably by himself.

As soon as he rounded a corner, he switched on the torch was switched on. He was surprised to find the corridor so clean and free from dust and cobwebs. Surely it hadn't been in use? They could have been rescued if that were true.

He knew that he was going uphill, for he felt the effort in his breathing as he walked. He had completely lost his sense of direction and could only surmise that he was going in the direction of the manor on the outskirts of the village. There were no doors right or left, only white tiled walls and ceiling. The floor was a pale quarry tiled affair.

If this corridor truly led to Tresaith Manor, he would have a good mile to walk and that would take him around fifteen minutes. He had remembered to note the time when he left the storeroom and 8 minutes had passed since then. His torch suddenly lit up double doors, blue in colour and metal in construction. These doors were firmly closed and seemingly secured by several means. Colin walked to them and tried opening bolts and chains. It appeared that the last person through the doors had done the final locking from the other side.

He banged on the doors and was rewarded with them shaking and rattling in response. He tried again and this time the doors just opened quietly, dragging a chain which had previously bound them together. Light flooded the corridor and Colin could see the gardens of

Tresaith Manor that he remembered well from his visit with Revie. He was still not near the manor house however. He stepped through the doorway and shut his eyes quickly as the sunshine momentarily blinded him.

"Jeez, I'm out," he muttered.

Aware that he may not be made hugely welcome by the Tresaith family, Colin turned away from the house and walked to the main gate of the asylum. The gates were closed and he nervously tried the bolt. It would not open and it didn't take Colin long to see that the padlock at one end was never going to allow him to open the bolt without the key.

Colin turned around in order to take in the view. He was going to have to climb the wall, he decided. Following up on this thought, he dragged a waste bin over to the birch tree and climbed. Within seconds he was atop the wall and looking towards Tresaith itself. There was nothing to help him down and he looked at the 20 feet drop. He watched the cars drive past and wondered briefly whether to hail one. But they would probably ignore him, he thought. He swung his legs over the top of the wall and closed his eyes as he jumped down. He felt a terrific thump vibrate through his body as he hit the ground. Colin thought he was going to vomit.

"What are you doing matey?" asked a familiar voice as he opened his eyes.

Colin answered wearily, "I've been trapped underground at Tresaith Asylum for months. There are a lot of people down there."

"Thanks for trying to give the game away Colin but sadly you are still trapped here, my friend."

Colin opened his eyes wide and engaged his brain.

"Trapped?"

Colin soon saw that he lying on the garden side of Tresaith Asylum. Jonny and George were looking at him in a concerned way.

"Yes. We told you that you can't escape this way. You are still the wrong side of the looking glass."

Colin got up and the three of them watched the gardener walking in their direction. Then they watched him pay them no attention whatsoever and stride in a purposeful way towards the shed.

"We are ghosts," said Colin. He was going to have to believe it now.

"I know! But not quite as you imagine, there will be a way back to your wonderful life outside the asylum, with all your friends."

"All my friends," repeated Colin. His only mates, chums and friends seem to be the people here at the hospital.

They walked back to the corridor and Jonny closed the doors behind him.

"I'm going to be stuck here for fucking ever," muttered Colin.

"Don't be so negative," laughed Jonny.

CHAPTER TWENTY

Later that night after supper, Jonny knocked on Colin's door.

"Do you fancy an adventure?" he asked.

Colin jumped up, "Yes," he answered.

"You will need your jacket, I've got the torches."

Colin was feeling excited about the prospect of an adventure – how pathetic was he these days?

The adventure took them up several stairwells until they were at the top of the clock tower. They had used torches to find their way to this point but now turned them off. Below them, apparently scurrying from building to building in the style of rats, were the group they had met in the outer yard earlier that day. The group held cameras and lights and did too much squealing.

"What are they doing?"

"Looking for ghosts."

"Are there other ghosts as well as us?"

"Not that I've seen," said Jonny.

The group looked up at the clock tower and Colin recognised the faces from before, particularly the woman. She pointed her camera directly at them and the ensuing flashing indicated that pictures were being taken. Jonny took some small stones from the floor and threw them through the open window at her. She flinched and screamed and the others ran to her. She continued taking pictures and Jonny threw some more stones.

"What's that in aid of?" asked Colin.

"Fun, you berk. Throw some at her friends."

"Because they can feel them? How come?"

"Inanimate objects. They are being propelled by us, so that's different."

Colin took some stones and threw one at the tallest man there. He ducked and reached up to his head, then looked at his hand and then up at the clock tower. The group walked to the door at the base and began ascending. Colin and Jonny could hear their footsteps on the pitch pine steps as they got closer.

"Should we hide?" Colin asked.

Jonny laughed for such a length of time that Colin considered it to be rude.

"No you twerp. Stay in plain sight and then you will see the glass barrier between us and them."

The group arrived in the clock tower room.

"It's really cold in here," said the woman.

"You're right and I've got this creepy feeling that we are being watched," said the tall man.

Jonny nudged Colin and showed him the piece of metal he held in his hand. Colin nodded and smiled as Jonny dragged it down the boards which partly covered the windows. The noise was enough to make fillings fall out.

"What the hell is that?" screeched another guy.

"It's the spirits of those who have past," said a man sagely.

"Well, you're the fucking psychic. Tell us who it is?"

"Idiot," said Jonny.

The psychic closed his eyes and ignored the clip round the ear which Jonny gave him.

"There is more than one person with us," said the psychic. "One of them thinks it's funny and the other is worried, I don't know what about though. There are two men and the joker is much older than the other man. One is a man in authority, the worried one. Perhaps he used to be in charge here or held a respected position."

Colin pulled a face and walked over to the psychic.

"Can you hear me? Can you really hear me? I'm Colin Buchanan. Detective Sergeant Colin Buchanan and I am trapped here somehow. I need help."

"He needs help I think," said the psychic.

"To pass over to the light?" asked the tall man.

"No, I don't want to pass over to the fucking light," shouted Colin. "I want to get back home!"

"He wants to go home," the psychic informed them.

"Definitely wants the light, Dave," said tall, then shouted. "Mate! If you can see the light, then go towards it!"

Colin smashed the torch from the tall man's hands and watched it roll across the floor.

"Steady on old man," laughed Jonny.

"He doesn't want the light," said psychic. "I think he wants to tell us something."

"I'm a policeman," shouted Colin.

"Talk normally," suggested Jonny.

"Colin Buchanan. My name is Detective Sergeant Colin Buchanan," he repeated in a more subdued voice.

"Detective, he's a detective. Might be a sergeant and I think he's Scottish," said Psychic Dave.

"He's pretty good this one," acknowledged Jonny. "Most of them are idiots."

"What's a Scottish detective doing in a North Wales nuthouse?" asked tall man.

"Perhaps he was an inmate," suggested a worried looking team member.

"I'm not an inmate! I was investigating and got lost and I want to go home," said Colin.

"You really want to get out of here, don't you?"

"I really do Jonny. I really do."

Jonny smiled and nodded.

"The detective is quite upset. I don't think he believes that he is dead," said Psychic Dave.

"You're not dead, Colin. Neither am I. Looking glass, remember?"

Colin was shaking and mentally trying not to fall into panic.

"Perhaps he's not dead," said the woman. "I've heard that people have slipped into a parallel universe in this place. There are loads of stories about it. For example…"

"You are talking bollocks Sarah."

"No I'm not. My mum worked here and they were always seeing ghosts but also they said that staff went missing and then turned up again weeks later. They wouldn't say where they had been and then one night someone told her that they had followed one of the nurses and saw her vanish through that room that you get to from the other side of the EST room. He couldn't follow her."

"Because the door was locked?" asked tall man.

"No, because she went through the wall, not the door."

"Was the EST machine being used at the time?" asked Psychic Dave.

"Couldn't tell you. But I do know that there was a patient in there."

"Who?"

"No idea. I can ask her."

"Do it," said tall.

"Plus, they sometimes thought that they saw people who had vanished looking out of windows like ghosts."

"Perhaps they were ghosts?"

"Can't have been, because they turned up again," said Sarah.

"I told you that there are spirits moving all over this hospital and they are pretty easy for me to speak to. And this guy is definitely a copper."

"Look at this," said Sarah. She was showing them the pictures on her camera that she had recently taken. The one she was pointing to showed Colin Buchanan peering from the clock tower window at her while she stood in the yard.

"That's me!" shouted Colin. "That's me!" He pointed at the camera and watched the picture die.

"What's happened?" asked tall.

"The battery has died," said Sarah. "I won't be able to do anything with it until we get back. I have no more batteries here."

"But it won't be lost?" asked Psychic Dave.

"Hopefully not. No, it should be OK."

"Please let it be OK," muttered Colin.

The group gathered their things together and made their way to the top step out of the tower.

Psychic Dave stopped. "That picture is important. We have to show it to the police."

"Christ Dave. That's mental," said Sarah.

They walked downstairs in the dark and Jonny and Colin followed them. The torches and camera lights belonging to the ghost hunters gradually died and they became frightened. Colin turned on his torch and soon realised that the light from that lit only his and Jonny's path and not the others. Colin began to feel sorry for them as they felt their tremulous way down the steps and he could hear their quickened breathing.

"They are following us," said Dave.

"I know," answered Sarah. "I'm frightened."

"No reason to be frightened. They don't mean us harm. They are just interested."

Jonny put a hand on Colin's shoulder.

"Let them go out on their own. We've had our fun."

Colin stopped and they waited until the group were out of sight.

"What happens now?" asked Colin.

"They'll either go home or try somewhere else on the site. I suspect they will go now, it's been too scary for them. They will be back. People always come back. They get addicted."

"Why are they wrecking the place though?"

"It gets done bit by bit. Come on one of these jaunts when the real druggie thugs come here. You might also see some of our more crazy rezzies attach themselves to them. That's real fun."

"I will."

CHAPTER TWENTY ONE

"Don't you ever get sick of this, boss?"

Roy Townsend was lying across his bed while Colin and a trustee nurse called Andrew were checking the room. Roy was reading a 15 year old newspaper and flicking it noisily when he turned the pages.

"Sick of what Roy?" asked Colin.

"Checking up on the rest of us. Just because you were a copper out there doesn't give you the right to apply the unlawful rules which Miss High and Mighty Tresaith chooses to invent."

"This is for everyone's safety Roy. You have been known to hide weapons in here," chipped in Andrew.

"Weapons? It's not Alcatraz you know. Though it might as well be, none of us can get out of this damned place can we?"

"I've heard that if you were to get out of here Roy, you would have to answer a few questions from my colleagues."

"So you say officer. There's a few more in here that are guilty of some serious shit. Take that Linda Jones. She killed both her parents, absolutely no question and she got Darren to help her. Then once he had sorted it out for her, she went and shot him too. Both of them got put in here to keep them out of prison."

"I'd like you to put that in a statement for me Roy. Then I can use it when I get out."

"Get out. You'll be lucky. I can write down all the stuff that Rob Parry has done to his wife too and that won't do you any good either. Face it boss, none of us are getting out."

Andrew held up a blue toothbrush which had its end chiselled into a point. "What were you going to do with this Roy?"

Roy stared at the offensive weapon and growled, "Shove it up your fucking arse the first chance I got."

"That's not very nice Roy. Plus it means that we will be checking you more often now." Colin took the toothbrush and put it into a plastic bag. He hadn't lost his form during the years of incarceration. One day he was going to solve all the troubles down here.

Roy shouted after them. "I know what happened at The Red Gable house too."

Colin stopped and turned round. "Like what?"

"I know who murdered them all and it wasn't anything to do with the old Commander Rutherford. He was framed."

"I've looked into that murder and it doesn't make any sense, I will agree to that. But how are you so sure?"

"Because I know Rutherford and he told me. He's one of the rezzies here and you know him too."

Colin was shocked and said, "That's shocking news. Who is he? I haven't met him."

"Oh yes you have and I'm not grassing him up. You find out for yourself. We all know that you were obsessed with that crime and would dearly love to know what happened. Hahaha."

Colin took a deep breath, deciding not to rise to the bait and smiled at Roy. He pushed Andrew out of the door and they locked it behind them.

Andrew said, "I don't know what he's talking about. No idea who he is talking about."

"I'll find out for myself."

"How are you going to do that?"

"Keep asking questions. It's the only sensible way to find anything out."

They walked together along the corridor, reaching the room which was occupied by Darren Jones. Colin knew something of his story from the records he had read and to this point had merely assumed that Darren had tried to kill himself. He told Andrew to continue on to the next cell.

"We are supposed to go in twos."

"We aren't far away from each other and can call for help. But I really don't think we need help with this lot, we know them all pretty well."

Two nurses came towards them and Colin called out, "If you ladies are not too busy you could help us out."

The nurses, who had formerly been patients, giggled at this exciting prospect and forgetting their original task, followed the men into their respective rooms.

"I just need you to stand at the door in case we need any help," Colin infirmed Gladwys.

"Yes sir. I can do that. Darren knows me though and he won't mind me being here."

"That's good Gladwys. Hello Darren, how are you today?"

"Just wondering Mr Buchanan how you suddenly seem to have such a lot of authority?"

Colin stopped. He had to agree that he had gone swiftly from panic stricken police officer to a man with the authority to move around the asylum as he wished.

"Just trying to help out here, there is a lot to sort out and too few staff. How are you feeling today?"

"Hungry actually, we don't seem to be getting as much food as we used to."

"True, but we had another delivery of food and medicine recently, so everything should soon be back on an even keel."

"You don't mean delivery Mr Buchanan. We all know that we can't get out and no one can get in. How did you get more food?"

"Found it. We discovered another store."

"Does it lead to a way out?"

"Not that we have seen so far."

"You have to have someone from the outside looking for you at the same place and the same time," said Darren.

"And during an eclipse?" asked Colin with heavy sarcasm.

"Or at midnight or during a thunderstorm or a heavy snow blizzard," answered Darren.

"I was joking and I assume that you are too."

"I think deep inside yourself, you know that I am right. Tell me, what was the weather like when you arrived here?"

Colin didn't have to think for long, "There was a bad thunderstorm, a very bad thunderstorm."

"Unusual weather and experiences of infrequent astronomical and chronological events encourage the veil to lift. It is of no coincidence that Tresaith and its Asylum is situated at the entrance to the largest vale in Wales."

"You are speaking as though you have some supernatural knowledge of the situation we find ourselves in," said Colin, with a little awe.

"I live in a shadow world now, Mr Policeman. I left the world due to an act of murderous intent by my cousin but was saved when I decided that I would not leave here and would haunt her for ever. That final thought and decision of mine catapulted me to a life between lives and the knowledge of the world was sitting there for me to find."

Colin had no answer to this strange speech and the nurse stared open mouthed at what she had heard. She broke the spell which seemed to hover over them when she said,

"Are you some kind of wizard Darren?"

"It depends what you think a wizard really is Gladwys."

"Someone what can cast spells and stuff?"

Darren laughed, "No, all I know is available to every living soul in the world if only they would determine to understand and listen. None of us ever die, we just jump from one dream to another and no one other than ourselves decides the next dream."

"You are saying that we never die?" asked Colin.

"No. We imagine that we moving towards death and some undetermined after life and all the time we are just dreaming and others think us dead and find some name to describe our death. They mourn us as if we are gone forever when all the time we have again recreated the dream life we just left and not noticed our own departure from the last dream. It is only when we are enlightened that we begin to create our lives in front of us because we are doing so consciously."

"If that is so, why are you not yet gone from here?"

"Because Colin, I am hoping to make a few more people understand before I leave here in a new Jaguar."

Colin laughed and sat down on the chair opposite the bed.

"I want to leave here Darren and if you have any advice for me in that regard, I would very much appreciate it."

Darren smiled, his face almost handsome now that his wounds were healing. "I have just told you. You must be ready to pass through the veil."

"And it's got to be during a storm or similar."

"Yes! If you are determined to get out, then you will. Most people down here think of this as their home and will spend many hundreds of years here before they realize they can escape."

"Surely they will notice the passage of time?"

"No one has yet, have they? You haven't noticed that you have been here a fucking sight longer than you think you have. The vast, vast majority of people think they are alive for a certain period of years and have not recognized that they die and are born again in every second of their life."

"Are you Jesus then?" asked Gladwys.

"No Gladwys. I'm not Jesus."

Colin left the room and told Gladwys to get on with her work. He had learned much more than he had expected. He leant against the corridor wall and for the first time in years craved for a cigarette, he needed to think about all he had heard. A familiar voice brought him back.

"Hello Colin. I haven't had time to thank you for your help finding us food and medicine and the rest. It will be a huge leap forward for us. I also hear that you have been watching the ghost hunters?"

"No problem on the first and yes I have on the second. I was just thinking that I might do it again, it passes the time if nothing else."

"Still want a way out then Colin?" Selina seemed disappointed.

"Of course I do. I want to go home."

"To your friends?"

"To my life and my career," he answered.

"Hmmmm. Well until we find out how that is to be achieved, there is a lot to be done around here. We still have patients to look after. Will you help?"

"Of course I will help. What do you want me to do?"

"Come to the EST room, I am going there now."

"Surely you don't still do that?"

"Of course we do! Why do you ask? It works very well!"

Colin was not convinced.

"A grandfather of mine was a doctor in an asylum somewhere and he didn't think that it had any positive results."

Which asylum was that Colin?"

"Not a clue. Scotland somewhere it must have been."

"What was his name?"

"Watson, he was my mother's father."

"There used to be a Watson here before me. I wonder if it was the same man?"

"Dunno. Doubt it. Maybe?"

"We'll look in the records when I'm finished here. That would be a coincidence," said Selina.

"Nothing surprises me anymore," thought Colin.

CHAPTER TWENTY TWO

As they made their way along the corridor, there was the familiar sound of rumbling wheels on the tiled floor. They instinctively moved to the wall and a small electric open cart trundled past towing twelve small trailers, each piled with meals in metal canisters. The driver tooted at them in thanks and disappeared around the corner on his way to the wards and private rooms. He would park it near the hairdressers at the far end and bring it back an hour later piled with dirty dishes and empty canisters. There he parked alongside the scullery and the dishes and canisters were removed there and placed in huge dishwashers where they would be made ready for the next meal. This was done four times a day, breakfast lunch, tea and supper.

"I'm glad we managed to find the new store Selina. But tell me, what will happen when that supply runs out?"

"Something will turn up Colin. It has to, doesn't it? I doubt we are all to starve to death."

"Shouldn't there be more of a concerted effort to find a way out?"

"Perhaps. However, I think that escape will bring a great deal of trouble to us all though, don't you see?"

"Perhaps it will be to you Selina and your family. It has been your decisions to keep these people away from the authorities."

"You are not thinking it through. Some of our patients will go to jail or another hospital where they will be alone as soon as the authorities know about them."

"Perhaps that is a better option than being locked away down here with a finite supply of food and medicine?"

Selina stopped, "Would it really Colin? Your experience in the force should be enough to convince you that any authority is more interested in its own survival than its clients."

Colin knew this was often true and so he didn't answer her. They walked in silence to the EST room and Colin suddenly recalled the words of the female ghost hunter. He asked,

"Has this kind of therapy changed much through the years?"

"EST you mean? Its perhaps kinder now than it used to be, but we still find it a very useful way to calm an otherwise distressed patient."

"How?"

"By applying electricity, I will give you an example. We had a woman who had suffered from panic, anxiety and many phobias for years. Drugs were only masking the problem and analysis was getting nowhere. Every day she had a hundred questions about her feelings and experiences and talked about her heavy heart and fluttering stomach. She would freeze on the spot sometimes believing most strongly that she couldn't move forward."

"That must have been terrible for her."

"I suppose but although she was in good physical health, she would not believe it and constantly recycled her thoughts which in turn recreated her nervous feelings."

"And you gave her EST?"

"We did and over several weeks."

"How did that improve her symptoms?"

"She forgot about them. She couldn't remember feeling as bad as she used to. She said to me at her next consultation, 'Doctor I am much improved since the shocks, I only have a slight fluttering in my stomach. What do you think is causing that?' This was a symptom she could handle."

"It sounds as though it was a doorway for her old feelings to eventually return."

"You are not a doctor, Colin. You don't understand."

"I know that understanding your symptoms is a huge step towards dealing with them and eventually curing them."

"There is no such thing as a cure. Management is the best we can aim for."

"So you are not familiar with the work of Dr. Claire Weekes? She had some incredible successes."

"I have heard of her but she is Australian."

"She has helped thousands of people."

"So you say. Well here we are." Selina opened the door with the authority all doctors demand and beckoned in Colin.

Lying on an examination table was Linda Jones, the woman who had been accused of shooting her cousin Darren, after killing her parents. She was naked and held down by leather straps, her arms stretched out as though she were on a cross. Her mouth was restricted by a ball gag and she wore a leather cap.

"She looks as though she is about to be executed."

"Nonsense. Nurse, that gag is not tight enough," instructed Selina.

This was soon remedied and Colin noticed that Linda's eyes were widening with horror.

"For God's sake, why is she naked?" asked Colin.

"Clothes interfere with the process. You are not excited at seeing a naked girl strapped down, are you Colin?"

"No, I'm not but where is the dignity?"

"Dignity? What dignity did she give her parents when she killed them?"

One of the nurses, a ridiculously large and stupid looking man began to walk over to him.

"Leave him alone Ron – for the moment."

Ron went back to his post by the machine and Selina busied herself with surgical instruments in a dish on a small table. The noise of her doing this was almost bringing on one of Colin's panic attacks but he wisely chose to ignore it. He didn't want to end up on the table like Miss Jones here.

"Stand back!" shouted another nurse and everyone responded. The noise from the EST machine was horrible - a snapping, crackling and smell. Like Frankenstein's machine, thought Colin.

Linda was gurgling and red faced as if she was trying to scream, but only spit and snot exited her nose from the effort. Colin could no longer stand it and went to the rear of the room pushing his body into the far wall. No one else appeared to notice that he was gone and so he slipped out of a side door. Inside it was cool and peaceful and the sound of another electric crack faded as soon as he closed the door. He put his hands to his face and almost began to cry before stopping himself in case he was heard.

The room he was in was small and empty save for a few shelves which housed a small box, a ledger of some kind and a clock. He picked up the ledger and leafed through it, noting that it had not been written in since the mid-1980's. He saw the signature of Dr. Watson – closer inspection proved that he was Dr. Colin Watson – Colin's grandfather.

He shut the book and put it inside his jacket. While his mind raced trying to assimilate this new piece of information, he sat on the floor. He looked around the room and his eyes soon rested on a far door. He thought of the woman's words and went to it. He was surprised and pleased when the door opened and he saw beyond it, the rear patient airing quad. It was deserted and tired looking and at the far end he saw boarded up doorways and piles of stones lying on the ground. This was the quad as he had seen it on his last venture outside on the food hunt.

He imagined at first that he could still hear the EST machine, but soon saw that he had stepped into a dark and foreboding thunderstorm.

Colin walked further out into the quad and breathed deeply. He saw a man leaning against the outer boundary wall, hand at his brow looking at the clock tower and he recognised him immediately as Lloyd Wright.

He shouted out and ran towards the doctor, thinking of him only as a way out of the mess he was in.

"Dr. Wright!" he shouted. "I am DS Buchanan, do you remember me? We last spoke over Skype! Are you here to free us?"

"Why should you think that, DS Buchanan? Freeing you and the nutters left at Tresaith Asylum will consign me to prison and that, my little blue bottle friend, is not going to happen."

Lloyd took a gun from his pocket and pointed it at Colin.

"Take me back in Buchanan. I need to see what has been happening during my absence."

PART FOUR

CHAPTER TWENTY THREE

They could hear Linda's screams from the shock treatment before they went back into the room.

Selina's face froze as she saw them enter and she stopped what she was doing.

"Lloyd! You are home! Thank God for that!"

She put down the electrodes she was holding and ran towards him and threw her arms around him. Colin noticed how pale Linda looked, while one of her eyes was swollen and bloody and vomit spilled down her front. The smell and the heat were unbearable and Colin found himself dry heaving into the sink.

Lloyd held his former colleague for only a moment, before he pushed her to one side.

"Linda still not responding to treatment then?"

"We keep trying, but as yet she has refused to acknowledge her sins," answered the nurse.

"I've missed all this Selina," said Lloyd. "The hospital in Canada is very modern and only uses drugs and psychotherapy. You have no idea how incredibly boring that can be in comparison to our treatments."

Colin wiped his mouth with tissue, listening to the talk around him. He was the most surprised to see how Selina had changed now that she was in the presence of Lloyd.

Colin had recently discovered during his gossips that Selina had worshipped Lloyd and that the affection was not reciprocated in any way. The scene to which he had just been witness, appeared to confirm that.

"Have you Lloyd? Have you really? It has been so quiet and lonely without you here. I hope we can bring everything back to normal." Then as though she has just noticed Colin, she said, "Where did you find him?"

Lloyd turned around and said, "Skulking in the airing yard. I think he was trying to escape and he imagined I would help him do it."

"He doesn't know you very well, does he?"

"It would seem not Selina."

Everyone in the room looked at Colin and he felt like Henry VI might have done when he saw his murderer arrive in his cell.

"I am still a police officer and if Dr. Wright can get in here, then clearly we can leave. I insist that you let me leave."

The group stared at him and Linda turned towards him. Her eyes were pleading with him.

"No one is stopping you Colin," said Selina.

"Just fuck off copper. No one will believe you," added Lloyd.

Colin turned around and left the room the same way he had done previously. No one stopped him. He made it out into the airing yard and into the storm. The yard was surrounded by high grey stone walls and asylum buildings whose doors would lead him directly back inside. He walked along all the walls, pushing at various intervals hoping for a doorway, but discovered nothing. He looked back to the EST room door to check there was no one following him. He turned handles on the doors of the asylum and none would open - bar one. He went in and discovered that he was in the kitchens.

He stood and took in the sights. There were huge stainless cabinets and cookers and fridge units and Colin realised that it was an almost exact replica of the kitchens downstairs. This had been vandalised like the rest of the asylum with writing on the walls and doors that had clearly not been written by his grandmother. There was broken glass and wood on the floor and empty alcohol cans lying around. He heard footsteps and so quickly moved into one of the large larders in case the intruder was – well he didn't know what, but he hid anyway.

A woman came into the kitchen carrying a camera. She was closely followed by two men. It was the same group he had seen in the clock tower.

"I'm sure I saw something or someone in here," said Sarah.

"I can feel a presence definitely," said Psychic Dave.

"Sure it's not your guide Dave?" Sarah and Chris looked at each other and smiled broadly. Dave was pretty good at his craft, but he really did make a meal of his 'Guide' and often brought her into play when he wasn't getting much response from spirits. The pressure was always on Dave because he charged for his services and results were expected. Today there had been nothing else on when Sarah had persuaded him to come to the Asylum yet again with the promise of twenty quid. He needed the cash as his benefits didn't stretch as far as his lifestyle and he was eager for the money. He had blamed his guide, Lily for keeping the spirits away and displayed a spectacular trance dance in order to demonstrate.

"Don't take the piss, Sarah. That doesn't help anyone. I am sure I can sense someone in here. It's a man and I think it is the man we saw in the clock tower."

"Lovely," said Sarah. "I rather fancied him when I saw his picture in detail."

Colin smiled from behind the door and then wondered whether he should come out and see if he could be seen, so to speak. But he remained where he was, leaning against a marble shelf which housed some pans.

"You in love with a ghost? Perhaps you will have better luck with a dead man than you do with a living one."

"Thanks for that Chris."

"Did you show anyone the picture?"

"I showed mum, but she didn't recognise him and so I'm going to put the picture in the next article I write."

"Did you show it to the police? He told me he was a copper."

"No, no I didn't. I wasn't really sure how to do it. I mean can you imagine them taking me seriously when I say, please look at this picture of a ghost who told us he was a policeman? I'd get locked up."

The others murmured in agreement, psychics and ghost hunters aren't generally listened to by the police. Colin quietly agreed with her. He would have dismissed any similar contact when he was – when he was what? In the police? Alive? He walked out into the kitchen as the group moved into the hallway. He was about to shout to them when he heard the most tremendous bellowing,

"What the hell are you lot doing in here? Get out of it, you are fucking trespassing." It was Selwyn, the caretaker.

"Selwyn, for God's sake. There's no need to speak to us like that. You know damn well why we are here."

"That I don't! You are always here looking for spooks and devils when you fucking know there are no such things!"

His shouting was accompanied by the sound of hysterical barking from his almost out of control German Shepherd which was straining at its lead.

"Selwyn, if that dog gets loose it's going to do us some damage and then you will be in serious trouble," Sarah was endeavouring to remain calm, because the dog clearly wasn't.

"Its private property, so I won't be in trouble," he assured them.

"Not so sure that applies in the eyes of the law, Selwyn. They'll end up putting the dog down and sending you to jail."

"The Tresaiths know what I'm doing here and it's their lawyers you will have to answer to. So fuck off!"

"Selwyn, leave us here to do our thing. I'm trying to write a book about ghosts and old buildings and if it takes off, I'll be able to look after mum."

Selwyn stopped shouting because he had a soft spot for Sarah's mother. It had been a hard spot for her when they were younger. He jerked the dog back and made him sit.

"You won't be able to use any of the pictures unless the Tresaiths give you permission and how likely is that? They don't want anyone knowing what has gone on here, do they?"

"Like what?"

"I could tell you stories about this place, about what used to happen with the unknowns."

"Unknowns?" Sarah was more interested than she was letting on.

"Buy me a drink and I might tell you! " Selwyn was tapping the side of his nose.

"I will. When and where?" Chris was ready to tie down their prey.

"The Dog, tonight and just for the record, I need some spending money!" Selwyn walked down the hallway laughing at his wit. His dog now relieved from his guard duties was trying to piss up the wall.

"He's such a fucking liar," said Sarah.

"Got to be worth a try though," said Dave.

Colin walked beside them and said, "I presume that you can see me now?"

Sarah, not generally a screamer, screamed.

"For fucks sake man! Where the hell did you come from?"

"You're the man in the photo!" said Sarah.

"I don't know anything about that," said Colin. "But I would sincerely appreciate a lift."

*

When he was explaining himself to DI Revie two hours later in his office, the story seemed far-fetched and ridiculous.

"Five years missing and you are telling me that you have been stuck in a parallel dimension with a load of missing people and the Tresaiths know about it?"

"They must do. Apart from that, Lloyd Wright arrived and I was able to leave."

"You should go and see the doctor and make sure everything is alright. Plus a visit to the police psychiatrist won't go amiss."

"I will. I intend to. But there's going to be a helluva lot to check up on, isn't there?"

"Yes, yes there is." Revie was finding it difficult to follow what he was hearing. If it hadn't been for the fact that he didn't think that Colin Buchanan had it in him to make stuff like this up, he might be more willing to believe that he had had a brainstorm and gone AWOL for the past few years.

"What's the next move?" asked Colin. He didn't really know what to do next. He had been desperate to leave the asylum and here he was speaking to his boss and knowing that there was no one to call and say, 'Stop worrying, I'm safe!' No one. What a fucking life he had built for himself.

"I told you. The doctor needs to see you and give you the once over. I need a report on that – well the bosses do. I don't care as long as you can work. Then a lift home for you."

"I still have a home then?"

"Oh yes. Your house is still there in Llangynhafal and has been looked after by someone called Alice Watson who says that she is your cousin. I believe that she is trying to prove through solicitors that she is your next of kin and have you declared dead. She hasn't had much success so far because I have had one of our tame solicitors block her progress. I always thought you would be back."

This news was unwelcome. Alice was a cow, a thieving lazy cow and a fat cow. He had never liked her even though she probably was his only living blood relative.

"Trying to steal my house? What about my salary? Seriously, I've been wondering whether I still got paid."

"It may have been on hold. I think it transferred to a pension or something which paid into your bank and paid your bills. But it would seem that your cousin has been getting the benefit of that. She moved in about a week after you vanished."

"Christ. I had better go and kick her out then."

"Don't be too mean Colin. She has kept the place going. It would have looked like Sleeping Beauty's castle if she hadn't."

"Perhaps that's true, I will be a gentleman. By the way, I want to go on any investigation at the Asylum."

"Doctor first and then the ACC will have to approve your return to work. Plus it seems that you have a lot to sort out of your personal stuff. We will investigate and let you know."

There appeared to be nothing more to say on the subject and Colin left Revie's office. Five years away and he didn't recognise most of the faces in the station. There were a few nods from some of the officers but no warm greetings. Perhaps they thought he had been making it all up.

"I have to take you to the doctor's surgery at Tresaith," said a young uniformed man at his side.

"Yes, thanks," said Colin and he followed him out into the car park.

The doctor's examination took only 30 minutes and he was declared fit and well, although a little tired and pale. The uniform took him back to Llangynhafal and drove off as soon as Colin had alighted. He took his house key from his pocket and walked up the path. The front garden at least was very neat and tidy, although Colin felt that it had been changed considerably. He turned his key in the lock and soon discovered that the key did not fit. He walked around the back and saw a fat woman hanging out washing.

"Can I help you?" she asked in a sharp voice. "You shouldn't really come round the back. This is private property."

"Yes, I know. It's my private property."

Alice carried on hanging and said nastily. "Back then are you?"

Colin felt like an intruder and took a deep breath in which he expelled slowly. He felt surprisingly wobbly and did not want to show it.

"So it seems. My key doesn't work in the front door."

"I've had the locks changed. I didn't want strangers coming in. I didn't know who you had given keys to." She walked ahead of him into the back kitchen and he meekly followed.

"Wipe your feet. I don't want your dirt in the house." She pointed to a mat.

He wiped his feet wondering when to bring to her attention that this was his fucking house and not hers.

"I suppose that you are expecting to sleep here tonight? Well, get that thought right out of your mind. I have been here for years and am in the process of having the deeds transferred to me. I have a solicitor on the case and for that reason I cannot allow you to stay here.

If it's your things you want, clothes and stuff, then they are in the garage. I packed them in cases. You are lucky that the things are still here, I was sending them to the charity shop when I got round to it."

Shaken at the ridiculous situation he found himself in, Colin said, "Alice, this is my house and my furniture. I am grateful that you have looked after it but I am here to tell you that you have to leave now. I am not dead nor am I missing, so you have to go."

"I am afraid that you are mistaken Colin. My solicitor tells me that I must stay here no matter what and you will have to leave. In fact, you must leave now or I shall call the police."

"Don't be stupid Alice. I am not saying that I won't give you a few days to get your things in order, but I am here to live now. I thought that you might have been more interested in what has happened to me."

"Not in the slightest," she said and left the room.

Colin looked around the living room and noticed that the only pieces left here were the valuable or antique. His comfortable leather chairs appeared to be missing and his Persian rugs were nowhere to be seen. Closer inspection of the other rooms told similar stories. His own bedroom had been commandeered by Alice and was covered in pink, purple and pale blue wallpaper and furnishings. He hated it. He was not a fan of supermarket décor.

The bathroom was changed. The bath was gone and had been replaced with a walk-in shower in avocado. Seriously – WTF?

He was having a pee, when he heard a car pull up in the rear drive. He lifted the small window by the handle and saw a police car and two uniforms get out. Alice was crying and shrieking and waving her arms in an animated way. The female officer looked up at the house and spoke on her radio. The male officer walked around the cottage to the kitchen door and shouted something which Colin could not hear. He finished the job in hand and went to the top of the stairs.

"Hello?" he said.

"Mr Buchanan? Could you come downstairs for me please?"

The officer was at the bottom and Colin noticed that he had his hand on his Taser.

"Certainly, I've only just been dropped off by PC err… something or other from St Asaph."

"I see. Can you please put your hands on top of your head for me? Thanks. Are you carrying a weapon of any kind?"

"No. Weapon? What sort of weapon? Of course not! What's the trouble officer?"

The officer stood away from the bottom step and pointed to the floor.

"Please stand here sir."

This Colin did and he watched the female officer join her colleague.

She said, "Miss Watson says that you have threatened her with a gun. Do you have a gun sir?"

"No! I haven't got a gun and I haven't threatened her! This is my house!"

"No it isn't! This is my house!" shrieked his cousin.

"Please get down on the floor sir," said the male officer.

"No! Why should I?" Colin felt his blood boil and dropped his arms. He was about to say something involving fuck and off when he felt a shock run through his body which knocked him from his feet and head first, shaking into the carpet. Colin thought irrationally that the carpet was a disgusting colour.

An hour later when he was being loaded into the back of an ambulance, Colin noticed three things. Firstly, the look of complete joy and triumph on the fat face of his cousin. Secondly, DCI Revie was there with a look of perfect anger as he shouted at the officers who had Tasered Colin. Thirdly, a beautiful woman with kind eyes and a smile he recognised from before he was lost down an asylum hole was talking to him. She was his neighbour and they had previously had no conversation other than hello and Bore Da and shallow sentences such as 'They said it wouldn't rain today!' She came over to him and said,

"If you want a witness to what happened when you got back or evidence of all that has happened since you went missing, then call me." She handed him a business card and he held on to it tightly.

"I have plenty of room at my house if you need to stay somewhere and keep an eye on your own place." She squeezed his hand and smiled again. Colin thought that he might cry.

He closed his eyes and heard Revie say, "If you had brains you would be fucking dangerous! He's one of us – a copper and a bloody good one!"

Colin spent the night at Bodelwyddan Hospital for observation. Revie had said he would visit during the evening, but never arrived. When Dr. Poole saw him the following morning, he said that Colin was fine to leave but must take it easy for a day or two.

"Do you have someone to collect you?" he asked.

"I will get a taxi," answered Colin.

"Can't one of your colleagues come for you?"

"They are busy, I think."

"Probably busy with the assault at Tresaith."

"Assault?"

"Some old boy was beaten up at a pub in Tresaith last night. He was really badly injured."

"Who? Do you know?"

"That old caretaker at the asylum, he probably upset one person too many. He falls out with anyone who goes there to take pictures or have an adventure."

"You know the asylum?"

"Only for sneaking in when I was younger. My dad used to do some doctoring there though and my mum was a nurse." Dr. Poole took the stethoscope from his ears and patted Colin's arm. Neither of them knew why.

"I could do with a chat sometime if I could, about Tresaith."

"Fine, I heard that you were lost while you were investigating it a few years ago? Is that right? How long were you, lost for?"

"Five years."

"Seriously? That's a story worth listening to. Now, do you want to phone someone to collect you?"

Colin handed him a business card.

*

When Helen Waters pulled up outside the hospital in her Range Rover, she leant across the passenger seat and threw open the door.

"Jump in! I don't want to pay for parking and that attendant has his beady eye on me. Look at him!"

Colin jumped in and she drove off. They were on the A55 before she said, "Where shall I take you?"

"Home of course!"

"I can take you to my home or to any other home you want. But I think until all the legalities are sorted out, it would be best not to return to your own home."

Colin turned to her and asked, "Why?"

"I just think it's for the best. Look, I don't know if this is appropriate to mention but I am a lawyer. Do you have someone acting on your behalf?"

"Revie said that he had a friendly police solicitor working on my behalf. I have no idea who it is and I don't know what they have done. Why? Would you help me?"

"If you like, I have a personal interest in the fact that I would rather you lived next door to me than – your cousin."

"So long as you are not too expensive."

"I shouldn't worry about that. If we play our cards right, you will be entitled to your salary, your pension plus a sizeable payoff for , well whatever trouble you were in. You will have to tell me about it, either as your lawyer or as your friend."

"I suppose. So, why can't I go home?"

"Because we need to have your cousin officially removed from your house first."

"Like a squatter?"

"Sort of, but perhaps she will move of her own accord."

They pulled up to Helen's house and had the satisfaction of watching Alice watching them.

"You go in," said Helen.

This he did and went into the porch from where he could see Helen stride over to the fence. There was a conversation which animated as it progressed but resulted in Helen being allowed into the garage of Colin's house. There were several trips back and to and soon cases and boxes were piled onto the lawn which Alice helped arrange. Colin was desperate to go out and help but stayed where he was until Alice vanished back into his house and slammed the door. It was only then that he went out and surveyed the pile.

"Your clothes and such," said Helen. "We can sort them here or the garage or your room, as you please."

"Are you sure about this?"

"Of course, you are in need of help and I can easily help. And I am more than a little desperate to know your story."

"Ok. Let's get this into the garage. I might have to throw some things away. I expect I will. I need to get a new mobile phone too."

"We can get that sorted. Look, I will help you take these things into the garage and then show you your room and leave you to it for a while. Help yourself to food and drink when you want."

"What did she say? Alice?"

"You don't want to know, she was a bit hysterical. I just said you were staying here for a while and haven't mentioned anything else. If I'm going to act for you – well I can't really."

Colin said nothing more. He couldn't think straight and wanted to sleep or rest or meditate or something.

*

When Colin finally woke, he looked at the clock on his wall and saw 12 o'clock. He couldn't work out what that meant and he couldn't work out where he was. He lay on his back and felt his mind try and catch up with his surroundings. He had already forgotten that he should allow his mind to decide his surroundings. It was quiet and the sun was shining through the window and he could hear sheep baaing. He sat up and felt dizzy and sick. He was dehydrated and he automatically reached for the drink he kept by his bed at the asylum. His hand touched a glass and he saw that it was empty but next to it was a small bottle of fizzy mineral water. There was also a note.

It was from Helen and informed him that she was at work and was going to have a look at his case and find out if anyone was representing him. Was that alright? Probably, thought Colin. No one else had been in touch. She said she would be back later and there was food and stuff in the fridge and she had left one of her old phones charging and he could find it on the kitchen table. She joked that she was aware that he would no idea how to use the IPhone properly but she would show him later. She would ring him around 12 and he ought to call his DCI Revie and find out what was happening.

That must have been what had woken him up. He remembered a strange and persistent noise that was not really a telephone ring. Colin got up, used the bathroom in all its capacities and came out in the dressing gown he had found hanging in his room. He went downstairs and looked at the screen of the phone which informed him that Helen had called. He filled the kettle and went to look out of the kitchen window. He saw his cousin in the garden, his garden and noted that she was staring at Helen's house.

"Bitch," he said.

The phone rang again and he saw that it was Helen again so he swiped the green phone signal in the direction of the arrow and said Hello.

"How are you feeling?"

"Weird. Woozy, I only just woke up."

"Good, sleep will do you good. Now make sure you eat, eat everything. I don't know what kind of diet you generally have, but there's fruit, vegetables, cereals and cake."

"I'll find something. Thank you."

"I've had a bit of a scout around and discovered that there is a solicitor working on your behalf from Conwy. Friend of the police but I know him too. Do you want me to find out what's happening? I can't do anything without your permission."

"Yes of course, please. You are being very kind."

"Not really, you can pay me back when I make you rich. I will see you later."

She put the phone down and Colin wondered why she was being so helpful. Any woman could have told him.

CHAPTER TWENTY FOUR

A month later, Colin was still living with Helen and still in a spare room. There had been plenty of opportunity to share but an unspoken agreement meant that, until his case was finished they would be nothing more than friends. Finally, Colin had a proper friend.

Once Helen had learned that Colin must attend retraining before being allowed back on active duty, she advised him to pursue compensation in the form of backdated salary, a decent pension and a large settlement. He agreed to this, especially impressed by the speed in which she was making sure that Alice was evicted and he would get his own house back. There was to be a court case next week at which she would almost certainly be served with a 30 day notice to leave.

"I never lose my cases," she told Colin.

He had a few meetings with Revie, who although was not supposed to be liaising with his former colleague was discussing the problem openly.

"The caretaker being attacked must be connected. He's not dead but not far off and he can't remember who did it or what happened. I think he does know and doesn't want to say and that's odd in itself. We aren't allowed to talk to him too much so haven't got a full story yet. I've had the asylum searched and checked out yet again and there is nothing to find except for worsening vandalism."

"You haven't found the way in like I told you?"

"No. Well, we found the door to the old EST room of course but no one has been in there other than the aforementioned vandals and ghostbusters since it closed. I'm not saying that you are mistaken because to be honest this whole thing is really weird. I've spoken to the Tresaiths and they tell me that the place has been closed down for years, they most definitely do not have a secret underground hospital where they keep old patients and that Selina Tresaith has been away for several years and they have no contact with her. They say she was a bit obsessed with Dr. Lloyd Wright and she may have gone to Canada to find him."

"They didn't mention any of this when we spoke to them back in … whenever the hell that was."

"No, they didn't. But a lot of time has gone by since then."

"You do believe me though?"

"There doesn't appear to be any reason for you to lie to me and you have no history of lying. Plus," Revie added before Colin exploded, "it all seems so far-fetched, that I don't understand why you want to lie to me. And I have no idea where you have been all this time."

"I've told you enough times. I wish I was making it all up. I sound crazy to myself."

"If the doctor hadn't told me not to take you, then I would ask you to come on another trip to the asylum and show me."

"I'll come with you. I'm not frightened anymore and I have no intention of getting lost again. When do you want to go?"

"Soon. It's a bit more difficult to get in there now without an appointment. Selwyn just met us with the key but now the owners have some sort of security firm with dogs and uniforms and they are making it difficult for us to get in, let alone any of these ghost hunter people."

"I wonder why they never did that before?"

"Money I'm assuming."

"Unless they think it is more likely that they will be found out now. They weren't bothered about the asylum being wrecked and I expect they considered that was a cover for their activities. Presumably you have checked the Tresaith finances?"

"We have and there is no record of any dodgy income over the past seven years and there are no available records prior to that. There was no obligation to keep them."

"No I suppose not. Have you asked the families of the people I saw down there? They must still be alive."

"Some are. But no one appeared to want to speak or said they knew nothing. Some were vaguely aware of solicitor organised trusts. As they are all moneyed families some with offshore accounts, it is impossible to check up on without a proper lead."

"What about Lloyd Wright?"

We checked on him and he is still in his Canadian job and there has been no sign of him leaving there for any length of time. It is true that he could have flown back to the UK under false documents for a short period of time, but so far we have no proof of that."

"I'm beginning to doubt myself now. Yet I know, I absolutely know what happened to me and have been recalling it all in excruciating detail."

"How are your sessions going?"

"Fine. She is good at her job and has never mentioned denial, repressions or strange voices in my head. Perhaps she is writing down a different report but I get the impression that she thinks I am going to be alright."

"Your lawyer friend Helen was a lucky find. I can't imagine her allowing anything to happen to you."

"She found me. I can't really remember knowing her before I got lost and since I get back I have been swept up by her."

"Is she a positive influence?" Revie asked tentatively. The office was dying to know what the situation was with Colin and Helen.

"I think so, I've known worse than her." Colin laughed. He was beginning to rely on Helen and so far she had not let him down. It was a comfortable feeling.

They decided to go back to the asylum the following day and Revie left his erstwhile colleague and drove back to base.

DCI Revie had initially searched the asylum to the point of panic once they realised that Colin was missing. The immediate team searched through the building for two hours and could find no sign. Eventually specialist services were brought in, including the local search and rescue team and not one clue was found. It seemed Colin had been seen by no one at the site or the town of Tresaith and nothing had been recorded of him anywhere until the day he turned up at the same place.

It had been assumed that he had fallen into one of the many shafts in the asylum grounds, some of which were known to be quite deep. Revie imagined that Colin would turn up one day, but that he would be dead.

They never had discovered who the four bodies were and so they had eventually been buried after all the usual tests and samples had been recorded. There were no clues pointing to anyone and gradually the case was filed away as other problems reared their heads. The vandalism continued and Revie would drive past sometimes and park in the layby on the other side of the stone wall and get out of his car and smoke. From this vantage point he could see the Gothic building in its faded glory. The clock tower stood centrally, keeping guard over the smaller buildings. It could have been a Victorian workhouse or school and Revie felt the presence of old ghosts working there. Sometimes he could almost see the old patients and staff at the windows or walking around the grounds and the guards at the gates. Everything he had heard about the place during his investigations had shown that it must have been a wonderful self-contained life for those who worked there. He wasn't so sure about the patients. Some of the treatments had been ghastly. However many Tresaithians had found love, employment and training there and they encouraged their children to work there too. It became impossible to get a job at Tresaith unless you had been introduced by someone who worked there already.

He would turn his gaze to the nurses' home, a long white building close to the north gate. The windows were smashed now and he knew that all the bedrooms and bathrooms were all but obliterated by vandals.

He would often see Selwyn walking around the site with his German Shepherd dogs which would viciously bark and snarl at the many intruders he would find wandering there. More visitors and vandalism had occurred since a live ghost hunting programme had been filmed there a few years ago and heightened the awareness of the asylum's existence to a wider audience. They exaggerated the treatments which had occurred there and announced proudly that the asylum was one of the most haunted places they had ever seen.

Revie often wondered on these smoke breaks whether he would see Colin's ghostly face at one of the smashed windows. But of course he never had.

Now when he listened to Colin's story, he believed him but had no idea how he would be able to prove it.

CHAPTER TWENTY FIVE

When Lloyd Wright and Selina allowed Colin to leave one nurse asked,

"What if he tells?"

"No one will believe him and the chances are that he won't be able to find his way out properly. I'm not worried," answered Lloyd.

Linda turned her head towards him, vomit streaming from her rigid mouth and her eyes showing terror. Lloyd smiled in return.

"You look as though you are still continuing with the outdated techniques Selina."

"My techniques work better than your lovey dovey ideas."

Lloyd laughed. "And what was that missing copper doing coming out of the building? I've been following the story on the internet about him and all the rubbish about ghosts. They have had his picture on one of their websites."

"Websites? You forget that we aren't as modern here as you are Lloyd. You come strolling in and out of here and brag about how advanced the upstairs world has become while we have been stuck down here."

"Can we come out yet Dr. Wright?" The nursing assistant sounded plaintive.

"Not yet, no. In fact, it's getting more difficult now." Lloyd nodded to Selina, indicating that he wanted to see her privately.

Selina put down the electrodes and said, "Clean her up and take her back to her room. I'll finish her tomorrow."

Selina washed her hands in the stone sink and waved them dry, choosing to ignore the towel. Lloyd looked at Selina and wondered why he had been talked into having that short affair with her. She often threatened to blackmail him with evidence of his collaboration in her family's' crimes. He wanted to find a way out, but was constantly drawn back to the hospital hoping that one day he would find the whole thing burnt to the ground and his problems solved. Lloyd followed different ghost hunting groups on social media and watched visits and heard about events at Tresaith Asylum. It was in this way that he saw different photographic evidence of assumed ghosts, where he recognised patients from his time there. He saw the picture of the policeman who he knew had gone missing on an investigation several years prior. He knew he must come back and sort the problem out for good. He had a good career in Saskatchewan and he wanted to remain there without the anchor of his previous existence.

Lloyd had been as shocked as he could be when he saw the policeman leaving the asylum as he arrived. And yet he knew that this would the only time that he would have been able to leave. Lloyd chose to ignore him, relying on the fact that with no evidence, few were likely to believe the copper.

He knew that it was highly unlikely that anyone else was going to find their way downstairs and what if they did? Well, he would deal with it properly this time. He may have to deal with the copper as it was because too much information out in the world wasn't really a good thing.

Selina was striding out in front of him and Lloyd found himself upping his pace. He could tell by the tension in her back that she was either cross or anxious. The visit would follow the same pattern, he knew. She would be reserved and discuss all that had happened since the last time she had seen him, like a professional. Then she would begin to swing her leg and ask him if he was seeing someone else and eventually she would scream at him, demanding that he do something about freeing them all. He thought that he probably hated her and yet they were tied together until one of them died.

"Shall we go to the office?" she asked.

"If you like."

"I forget how dark and dank it is down here," he said.

"It just feels normal to me," Selina answered.

"I suppose it would," Lloyd answered.

"So are you here to check up on me or have you found our route to freedom?"

"No route to freedom, unless you leave and hide. I tell you every time I come that the world has moved on so much since we stayed here that we can't just sneak people out."

"Did you go and see the family? We almost starved you know. It was only because some of the patients and that copper managed to find another storeroom. But we are running against a brick wall now. We have come to the end."

"The family wouldn't see me and wouldn't let me see Carys either."

"Did you find out how she was?" There was little emotion attached to the question.

"I found out nothing. One of the staff answered the door and I didn't get further than that. If I made a song and dance then I imagine that the police would have been called."

"She will be better with my family there. Good schooling and a good career will set her up. We can't offer her anything."

Lloyd didn't tell her that he had been writing to Carys for several years now that she was able to communicate. He hadn't told his daughter the entire truth naturally, but soon discovered that Carys was more than willing to have a relationship with her father. She believed that her mother was ill, living in Canada and currently unable to write to her daughter. Carys was not particularly happy with her Tresaith relatives despite their care of her. She soon began to believe in her badly done to parents, expelled from the family home and denied their rights. Keeping a secret such as this was positively delicious for her.

"I would like to have my daughter with me. I miss her, don't you?"

"Not really. I don't like girls, I wanted a boy."

Lloyd didn't answer. He never answered when it got like this. He thought back to his first wife and the way she had died. Too many times since his time with Selina had he been suspicious of Selina's treatment of his late wife. Eventually he surmised that Selina had killed her, but of course by then she was pregnant with Carys and he could do little about it.

Eventually though...

"Any more problems? No more bodies to dispose of badly?"

"No. That is, we have had three more deaths but this time we buried them under the slabs so no one can find them."

"Natural deaths?"

"Two of them were. One I'm not so sure about, Roy Townsend was involved and you know what he is like. It was Phyllis and she was acting as his nurse."

"The trouble is that we are getting more deaths now and..."

"And we didn't used to get any at all. They are beginning to realise that there is a limit to their lives."

"So, soon they will start dropping off their perches. That might actually be a good thing."

Selina looked at him with contempt.

"These people are my patients Lloyd. I have been around them for so many years now and I don't want them to die."

Lloyd knew that she meant she liked having power over them and would not give up that power easily.

"There won't be a way out with them Selina. You know that. You either have to find some way to stay here with them or leave without them.

"You are always saying that and I am always saying that if you don't help me I will make sure that everyone knows about your predilections."

Lloyd was going to have to get rid of Selina.

"Do you want to pay a visit to some of your own patients? None of them have died?"

Selina laughed and walked out of her office, carrying keys. Lloyd followed her. They reached a familiar green door and Selina put the key in the lock and turned it. She beckoned him inside.

"I will give you an hour," she said.

Lloyd walked inside and saw Gill lying on her bed in a white lace nightgown. She was as beautiful as she had always been. Gill had been sent to the asylum during the Second World War following a dalliance with an American airman and the resulting pregnancy was enough for her landed family to have her committed. Her son had been taken from her at birth by the asylum doctors and returned to Gill's mother who raised him as her own son. This son, the only blood son the family had, inherited their substantial properties and his son became as prominent as the family had always been. He knew about the asylum and its secrets, for he was friends with the Tresaiths and they were all members of the same Lodge.

"Oh Charlie! You came back! I was so frightened that you might have been shot down or kidnapped and in a prison camp."

"I told you I would be back as soon as I could. How are they treating you?"

She got up from the bed and hugged him before kissing him so lightly.

"They treat me very well. Will I be leaving here soon? I want to see our baby boy."

"You will see him soon Gill, you just need to look after yourself for a little longer and then you can come home."

"My mother will let me come home now? She has forgiven me?"

"Of course. Now they know that we are to be married, they are happy and will let you come home."

"Oh Charlie, I love you so much." She kissed him and pulled him towards her and they fell on the bed as they did every time he came back. Lloyd knew that he was as bad as Selina as he undressed and began to fuck Gill.

He was asleep when Selina came back into the room and shook him.

"Never waste any time, do you?"

Lloyd opened his eyes and saw that Gill was still sleeping. Only this time, he noticed how old she was looking. She was bent and small and shrivelled and her straggly grey hair was ill kempt and dirty. She looked like the hospitalised and uncared for 85 year old woman that she was. Gill woke and turned to her lover and smiled a toothless hag smile. Lloyd had colleagues her age and older and they didn't look like Gill but he certainly didn't want to fuck them.

"See what I mean Lloyd? They are all changing. Imagine what the original lot are going to be looking like soon."

Lloyd was retching into a basket at the corner of the room. He had just fucked an old lady for Christ's sake.

"You won't be doing that again will you?" said Selina smugly.

CHAPTER TWENTY SIX

Lloyd had one hand on the wall of the hospital corridor, his coat in his other hand and was still retching.

"Jeez Lloyd, I didn't have you down as such a baby."

"Did you know? Did you know she would suddenly age like that?"

"They are all doing it at different times and then back to their original selves. But the true age look is becoming more regular and I expect will be permanent before long."

"But you knew it was likely? Why didn't you tell me?"

"You once told me that we all learn best by doing rather than hearing." Selina was smiling.

"You are a fucking bitch Selina. I hate you."

Selina seemed pleased at this remark, giggling as she walked in front of him towards the wards.

Lloyd staggered behind her making plans in his mind.

"Aren't you worried the copper is going to tell? We are all in the cart if he does."

"He spent most of the time drugged up and asleep and didn't see most of what went on. He doesn't know that he was sedated for days and weeks at a time and particularly throughout the stuff he didn't need to know. I expect he has a very scrambled mind now and people aren't going to pay too much attention to what he says."

"But they will know that he spent his time down here, won't they?"

"Will they? I'm not so sure. Perhaps you should put about that he was off somewhere else. Perhaps you should kill him."

Lloyd didn't answer. He wasn't going to tell anyone that he came down here to visit. He never did that ever, to do so would be an end to his long term goals.

They arrived at the crossroads of corridors where to turn right took them to the main female ward and to turn left was the male ward. The exact equivalent upstairs had been called Piccadilly due to the amount of people traffic there had been there. The corridors also led to the main hall, either used for sports or social and theatrical events. There was the surgery, the dentist, the hairdressers and the corridor to the mortuary and the work offices and the dairy. The list was endless. Downstairs it was still called Piccadilly, but the traffic was nowhere near the same.

They turned towards the female wards.

"They will be pleased to see you Lloyd."

He smiled as he entered the swing doors and looked at the beds lining the walls. He was used to seeing women of all types, short, tall, blonde, brunette, slim and voluptuous. He had enjoyed himself every day he had been here after the place had closed upstairs. Then, he had been on his best professional behaviour, but the temptation which came to him as soon as there were no checks or visits or reports to write meant that he had gradually fallen into bad ways.

Initially he had wanted to quietly test out his theories that orgasm through either masturbation or full sex with another party was an excellent way to improve or cure the symptoms of female anxiety. It had been a popular treatment during Victorian times for hysteria and feminine independence, losing popularity during the following years until it had almost died out in the 50's.

Lloyd had argued its case in some of his papers where he mentioned that he knew some doctors who still believed that clitoridectomies were a valid way forward. He had never imagined that he would have chance to test his theories in a valid format, but when Selina had discovered his work she insisted that he practice it at Tresaith.

"We needn't tell anyone else until your work is complete. Then you can publish and make a name for yourself."

It had all sounded so feasible and tempting – a fellow doctor encouraging him in his theories. Soon he was treating some of the women, the younger prettier ones naturally. Their consent was not required and no nurse would question him, they had been patients before the asylum closed down. Doctor always knew best.

He would make the women undress and examine them thoroughly with his gentle light touch. Sometimes Selina would accompany him and watch and encourage. The examinations turned to massage and then he would manually stimulate their naked bodies with his oiled fingers. Most of the women enjoyed what was happening to them and soon formed a close bond with their Dr. Wright. A few of the more enlightened women would object in strong terms at this disgusting treatment and so Selina would have them strapped to the examination bed while Lloyd stimulated them anyway. At least 50% of these tied and objecting women would climax involuntarily as their bodies answered the mechanical requests. Neither Selina nor Lloyd seemed to care that adding this guilt to their already confused minds would set their minds even further back down a hole. Lloyd had also persuaded the loveliest of the women that sucking his erect penis while he masturbated them was only adding to their successful treatment.

It didn't take long before he had forgotten his original intentions and just enjoyed it all for its own sake. It was why he would now return so often. A few weeks of regular BJ's and hot women would set him right to go back to Canada. Selina didn't appear to mind. He knew that she knew that he wouldn't come back at all if it wasn't for this.

They strode into the ward and Lloyd waited for the oohs and squeals as he walked in. He smiled his broad smile in anticipation.

But there was something wrong. The only noise he could hear was repetitive speech such as, "My name is Barbara you know, I'm only 54," repeated ad nauseam. "Where's my tea nurse? I haven't eaten for hours," followed by groans and grunts.

And the smell! It was a disgusting mix of old food, pee and shit mixed with a fragrant mustiness. Just like one of the badly maintained EMI units he needed to visit from his Canadian practice. Where were the hot women? Where were the young girls?

"Surprised are you Lloyd? I told you it's all falling in on us. Something has got to be done."

"Fucking hell," was his answer.

"Don't fancy doing some treatments while you are here?" she asked him.

"Not fucking likely. What about the men's ward?"

"I will take you there but basically it's the same as this. We have a few left who don't seem affected and I think that's because they are all in their own rooms. I worry that if they cross paths with the main wards that they will go down the same route. It's as though an aging virus has hit them all during these past weeks."

"What about Jonny and George and Joseph? Are they OK?" Lloyd had had some adventures with that trio. He hoped they hadn't changed.

"Just the same, literally just the same. They don't seem to have been affected. They spent a lot of time knocking about with Colin," she added.

"Colin?"

"The policeman who was here."

"Yeah, I wanted to ask you about that. What was his story? I mean how did he end up here?"

"It was one of the searches that the police did after they found the bodies in the mortuary. He had some sort of seizure when he was at one of the portal doors and nearly died. So he was seen and carried through into here. Technically, he was lucky because he would have died out there if we hadn't brought him in here."

"Does he know that?"

"I don't think he can remember what happened. Like I said, I kept him drugged most of the time so he only has half a story, well probably a tenth of a story. He won't be able to piece it all together. He thinks he has remembered everything that happened, but he hasn't. I expect his mind will cave in on him in about five years' time."

Selina thought about the time Colin had arrived. Joseph and Phyllis had seen the police doing another search. Everyone liked to mess around with the ghost hunters and the trespassers, half appearing and making whoo-whoo noises that would scare them half to death. But the patients could only be seen fleetingly before they disappeared back downstairs. On one or two occasions a visitor had fainted or got so drunk that they passed out and in that state they were more aware of the downstairs people. Some of the more challenging patients had been able to attach themselves to the more vulnerable and the more outrageous interlopers. In this way they had been able to persuade their hosts to damage and smash the old asylum up. These patients were not pleased about the way they were treated and vented their frustration on the building via these interlopers.

Selina had always thought that it was something to do with this mixing with the outside world that had brought the aging virus to Tresaith. There was no obvious way to prove it, but everything fit with the theory. What it did mean however was that the end was coming - the end to her fantasies, her control and her ability to indulge in her peccadillos. Leaving here meant that she would never be able to do the things she enjoyed doing with complete immunity. Leaving here might mean that she would have to face up to the demons inside her mind that were driving her to abuse others.

"You had better hope he doesn't, otherwise the roof is coming in on both of us."

"That can't happen and you know it."

Selina thought about Darren. She had felt so bad for him when he came in with his shot face. They knew the truth of the matter - the fact that Linda had shot Darren in order to keep him quiet about her own murderous deeds had enraged Selina. She remembered Darren coming to the town with his mother and how sweet he had been. She remembered how she had always considered Linda a conniving bitch. They had hated each other during the short association they had had prior to Linda arriving at the asylum. Darren had told Selina during therapy about Linda's plan to murder her parents and frame her father so that she could get the farm and all its lands to herself. It was then that Selina decided to increase the therapy on Linda.

She started out with drugs, test driving some new hallucinatory concoctions which hadn't completed their field trials. Some of the responses would have been alarming if prescribed ethically. But Selina considered it fun. She had encouraged Lloyd with his desire for his theories and experiments and said she would support him as long as he supported her. She wanted to try the now discredited clitoridectomies, believing that rampant female sexual desire was at the root of their anxiety. A psychologist might say that this was a result of her Tresaith influences and her early sexual assaults. Selina thought it was a way to ensure that she kept Lloyd's interest while allowing his rapidly degenerating experiments. There was no way that she was losing him. No way.

Linda was the first woman on whom she performed the clitoridectomey and she did it out of spite. Linda was only hospitalised by paternal relatives in order to save the family name and also return the farm to them. As they were also Darren's blood relatives, they knew the real story and wanted the whole lot brushed under the carpet. No one was going to benefit from an investigation.

Linda didn't know she was going in for an operation such as this. Selina told her that she was going to have her wisdom teeth removed under anaesthetic. When she came round she went apoplectic and proved her apparent paranoid behaviour which had resulted in the murders of her parents. Linda was a psychopath not a paranoid and she knew that whatever Selina did to her, she would return in spades. Spat after spat resulted in the special EST treatments, of which Selina was so proud.

When Selina thought that Lloyd was becoming particularly attached to one of his pretty patients then that patient became the next candidate for Selina. This was soon noticed and dismissed by Lloyd as another example of her silly ways. There were plenty more fish in the... nuts in the nuthouse.

If either Selina or Lloyd had begun their careers with an intention to do good for those with mental challenges, their life within the poisoned walls of Tresaith Asylum soon altered that. Neither were good people.

"Here we are," said Selina as she opened the door.

It was the same here as the female ward. Lloyd noticed that some of the men were more active and aware than the others, who lay in their beds and were apparently pissing themselves to sleep.

"I'm not staying here," said Lloyd and turned on his heels.

Selina laughed, closed the door and followed him out. As if the scales were falling from his eyes, Lloyd noticed the peeling paint on the walls and the dust and dirt everywhere. Broken floor tiles and a couple of doors hanging from their hinges showed him that this downstairs asylum had degenerated much further than he had ever noticed before.

Yea – the end had come.

CHAPTER TWENTY SEVEN

"So this is definitely where you came out?"

Helen was with Colin and DCI Revie and Gwen Hughes. This trip wasn't an official evidential investigation as there wasn't judged to be anything substantial to investigate. Colin may or may not have been in the asylum for the past five years, but several searches on the back of the ten searches which had taken place during his absence had revealed nothing. He may have suffered from amnesia or been with a lover and now decided to return, no one could tell. The force did not want to answer the dereliction of duty case in regard to Sergeant Buchanan threatened by Helen and so had agreed to the final payment and pension package she had presented them with.

Revie still had a feeling about the whole case and when he talked to Gwen one day, she said that she wouldn't mind coming back to the asylum, so long as they went in the daylight.

"Bright, middle of the day daylight where we all have radios, telephones and megaphones if necessary," she had insisted.

"Would you like that we all hold hands?"

"I wish you were being serious, because I think I would rather we all held hands."

Helen was coming because she was Colin's lawyer and had an interest in all aspects of the case. Plus Colin was beginning to rely on her a lot, perhaps too much. He had found that the longer he had been out of the asylum his anxiety was a constant companion, often exploding into full blown panic when he was at his most vulnerable. Helen was the crutch he needed for the time being. She was helpful in every aspect of his life and had already started referring to them as 'us and we.' Colin wasn't sure if he liked it or not but he did need it.

"This is definitely the way I came out. The northern airing yard and this door led directly into the EST room although I agree it doesn't make any sense."

"Not least because it's on a different level," said Helen.

"And it's getting in a worse condition every time we come here," said Revie.

"But if the entrance is on a different level in terms of spiritually, we wouldn't see it would we?" Gwen could voice her opinions more openly now that she was no longer in the police.

Helen and Revie looked at her witheringly, while Colin smiled a grateful smile.

"So how do you want this search to work Colin?"

"I know it will be a waste of time to just go through the place again randomly. I think we should visit the stairwell where I first got through and the areas where I came out on my travels during my time there. So that will be the clock tower and the quad near the main hall behind the clock tower. Oh and the south side that goes towards Tresaith Manor."

"Shall we just follow while you lead the way?" asked Revie.

Colin suddenly looked vulnerable and became breathless and pale, but continued.

"If you like, I mean you can go and investigate any part of the hospital but we are here to find a way down aren't we?"

"Yes we are," said Helen as she grabbed his arm and supported him as though he were going to collapse.

Without realising he had done it, Colin pulled his arm away from her and insisted, "I'm fine. I've got this."

"I didn't want you to have one of your spells again," she said, obviously hurt.

Gwen interrupted. "He looks fine to me Helen. I remember when I had been in hospital for months after a riding accident. I broke my pelvis and my back and... well, it doesn't matter about that. What I mean to say is that when I came out, I felt really wobbly and anxious out in the supposed real world for quite a few weeks. I found that once I accepted that it was a normal reaction and would just wear off as soon as I stopped worrying about my worrying so to speak. Well – I just got better." She stopped, flushed from her confession.

"Thanks Gwen," said Colin. "That means a lot." Colin stood taller and led them to the front of the asylum where he ran up the main steps to the heavy wooden front door. This had now been reinforced in a similar manner to the rest of the asylum in a vain attempt to deter the hooligans and the trespassers. The only people it actually kept out were the honest ones, for the other lot just ignored the doors and smashed the windows and went in that way instead.

They had been warned about the floors here, which were no so rotten and wrecked that they could give way at any time. They agreed to walk around the edges wherever they had the chance to limit the problem.

"It seems to have got even worse since Selwyn has not been around scaring everyone away."

"Poor guy, how is he?" asked Colin.

"Still in a coma, they don't know if he will make it. Someone did a proper job on him," said Revie.

"Oh no! At least his dogs are being looked after though. His brother has a farm at Prion and has put them in the kennels and they have a massive run there. They are quite happy," Gwen told the group. Only Helen appeared disinterested.

"Good job they got some proper security in," she said. "Instead of leaving it to a dopey old codger."

No one answered. Two of the group did not want to offend Colin and Colin wanted suddenly to tell her to fuck off. He was feeling stronger now that he was here again. Here, he had had friends.

The door was opened and they went in.

"What a shame!" cried Gwen, echoing the thoughts of every decent person who had entered the building since its evacuation.

It seemed as though the place had been deserted for about a century and the signage and furniture and anything that wasn't nailed down had been taken. Colin corrected that thought. Even the nailed down stuff had been taken.

"If we go through this way..." he led them to the left of the reception area. "And go down here, the stairway leads up the tower."

"Why don't we just go upstairs using the main staircase?" asked Revie.

"Because I went this way with Jonny and George up the clock tower and I want to see if there is any evidence of that."

"But it's not the way to the area you were? That was downstairs?"

"Yes boss."

They all walked carefully up the spiralling oak and stone steps fanning out from a central stone column. There was room for only one person on each step, enhancing the claustrophobic feeling for each of them. Colin noticed it first and turned round to Helen in case she was considering grabbing him again. Helen was looking at her feet, apparently sulking. Gwen, stepping behind Helen winked at Colin and he grinned and turned back to keep an eye on the way ahead.

"Are we nearly there yet Colin?" asked Revie, who was bringing up the rear and puffing a lot.

"Not far now," Colin answered and climbed over the top step to bring them into the room there.

The group spread out and looked admiringly around the room and out of the broken windows to the courtyard at the back and the front drive on the other side.

Colin looked out too, remembering when he had seen the ghostbusters first. It didn't feel as though there was a different atmosphere here today – now that he was on the other side of the veil.

"I was in here with some of the patients one time and some ghostbusters arrived with their cameras and stuff. The thing was, we could see and hear them and they couldn't see us."

"They weren't pretending?" asked Revie.

"Why would they pretend? You've interviewed them haven't you? Did they say they could see us? "

"I haven't interviewed them."

"Really? I said that they were supposed to meet with Selwyn the night he got beaten up."

"I'll ask. Someone must have spoken to them, I'm not particularly involved in that case. They wanted other officers to deal with it."

"They had some psychic with them and he could hear me and was passing on the messages."

"Psychics are all fakes," announced Helen.

"They are not, not this guy anyway. He heard me."

Helen knew she was being snappy and didn't care. She had done a lot for Colin and was happy to do it. A single woman, she found it almost impossible to meet a decent man. She had seen Colin before he went missing but thought little of it. He was just a neighbour. She had been having an affair with a partner at her law firm and was involved in all the manoeuvres that brought with it. That had split acrimoniously not long before Colin returned and she had enjoyed all the challenges involved in getting Colin the right result. She also found him very attractive and it didn't do her ego or reputation any harm to be seen around the locality with Colin at the meetings and the investigations. It had been noted at her firm and there was a good chance she would be getting some good cases on the back of it. Soon Colin would be able to return to his own house and she found that she was quite pleased about the prospect.

Paul wanted her to get back with him and he had been persuading her with renewed promises of leaving his wife – as soon as the children had finished university.

Paul could do more for her career than Colin was able to and she still loved him.

Her problem was how to tell Colin without losing the ability to finish his case. He wasn't paying her as such but it wouldn't do her any good to bail out early.

"Perhaps we should speak to him," said Gwen.

"We should. I'll see about that back at the office," said Revie. It was a shame that Gwen didn't work with him anymore.

"Come on everyone. We had better crack on," said Colin and he skipped back down stairs. He led them to the southern airing yard and then around the southern side of the oldest part of the asylum until they found the doors he had gone through on their food hunting adventure. They were hidden behind brambles and nettles and elder. Colin used a stick and bashed down as much as he could. The doors were revealed and there was an advanced selection of bolts and chains keeping them shut.

"We need to go through here," said Colin, slowly turning one of the padlocks.

"I've got some serious bolt cutters in the car," said Revie. "Shall I get them?"

"If you don't, I will," said Gwen. She was having fun.

"This is taking longer than I thought it would Colin, I'm going to have to leave," said Helen. "Will you be alright for a lift?"

"Yea sure," he answered.

"I'll take him back," Gwen interrupted.

Helen walked back to the cars with Revie, so Gwen and Colin were left alone.

"It's totally none of my business, Colin. But what the fuck are you doing with her?"

"I'm not really with her – with her – if you know what I mean."

"I think so…" she answered carefully.

"She helped me immediately and then has been very helpful since. I don't think that I would have been so far ahead with my property and my settlement without her single minded dedication."

"I'm not so sure about that. You could have used the Police Fed."

"I suppose so. I did suggest it but Helen said that it would be better if…"

"Have you signed anything about your settlement?"

"No."

"Well, have a word with the rep first. She's very fair and discreet.

"Anyway that's why I'm involved with Helen and the fact she gave me a place to live right next door to my own house sort of nailed it."

 "Do you love her?"

"Christ no!" he answered a little too quickly and Gwen laughed.

"So what will happen when you are back in your own house?"

"Not sure. I hope I don't have to end up selling it. I hope it doesn't end up being awkward." His voice tailed off. He was voicing ignored internal mind rumblings and seeing that he was grateful to Helen and that was it. He was saved when they heard Revie's car draw up.

"Didn't see the point of walking all the way back when there is a driveway. Helen's gone off – she's a bit - err intense when she wants, isn't she?"

Gwen smiled and Colin shrugged. Did no one like her then? He felt as though he was thinking more clearly than he had done since he escaped the asylum and as though the time in between had been foggy.

Revie opened the boot and the three of them took tools and made their way towards the doors. It took almost half an hour but they eventually had all the bolts and chains undone and the doors dragged open. A pigeon flew at them, skimmed their heads and flew into the distance.

"You know that's the first bird I think I've seen here," said Gwen. "Usually there are birds everywhere at any place, particularly when there are so many trees around."

"That's true. I haven't seen any evidence of birds or flies or bees... I never thought about it before."

There wasn't time to think about it now. Three people walked through the asylum doors, looking right, left and in front in the style of their police training, former and current.

Colin recognised the journey from his prior trip and led the group, though only slightly ahead of them. The corridor was the same as when he traversed it with Jonny and George although there was no sign of people. No one at all. None of the three spoke, all a little anxious as they travelled further from the safety of the outside door. The passed the doors which Colin believed led to the discovered storeroom but these refused to open when rattled. They carried on their way until they arrived at the bottom of a set of stairs. Colin climbed up first and levered the trap door open, beckoning the other two to follow him.

There was no one in the cobbler's shop, but it seemed that someone had been there recently. A cold half-drunk cup of coffee sat on the table accompanying two pieces of toast, both of which had had large bites taken from them. A scoop of marmalade lay next to these, having been ignored by the meal taker. Colin recognised this as the kind of meal he had eaten many times during his incarceration. They must be on the right track or in the right universe at any rate.

He opened the cobbler's shop door and they stood in the courtyard and this time there were people. Patients and nurses moved around in the corridors as they looked at the windows of the hospital, the same windows that had been dark and empty only hour ago.

"Fuckety fuck fuck," said Revie eloquently.

"Have we gone back in time?" asked Gwen tremulously.

"I told you I wasn't making that stuff up," said Colin.

"What's your plan now?" asked Revie.

"I don't have one. I was so busy trying to prove I had lived in another part of the asylum for five years that I didn't imagine what I would do when I arrived back."

"I think we should go straight back in case there is some kind of time lock on the door," said Gwen.

"Like a five year time lock?" chuckled Colin.

"I fucking hope not," said Revie grimly. He wasn't feeling very comfortable.

Selina Tresaith was striding towards them.

"Colin!" she sounded surprised. "I didn't expect to see you back here after you discharged yourself."

"Yeah, whatever you say. Look, this is Detective Chief Inspector Revie and err Gwen Hughes. We came to find you and…"

"See if it was all for real? What do you think?"

"I would like to have a look around before we return," said Revie. He put the emphasis on return, he was in a space now which none of his substantial training had prepared him for.

"I am sure you would Mr Revie. And I also think that you need a warrant but we both know that is not really a possibility."

"We could go and get a warrant if that would make you feel easier," said Revie, sensing danger.

"You won't be going back anywhere Mr Revie," said a man holding a gun to his head. "Hi Colin!" he said. "You shouldn't really have come back."

"I am thinking that myself, Jonny."

"The sensible move would be to abandon your colleagues here and re-join our merry band, Colin."

Colin grinned. This was getting tricky but he didn't want to antagonise anyone. His police training was kicking in.

"How is that going to work out Jonny? Why don't we both allow ourselves to travel freely wherever we want to go?"

"It isn't possible is it, Colin?"

"I've learned how to do it. I have been out and I've come back in and I can show you how."

Jonny lowered his gun slightly.

"Really Colin? Could I go home? Is it possible?"

Colin took a step towards Jonny and said, "I've done it."

"If you take one more step Mr Buchanan, I will shoot you myself." Lloyd Wright was holding a shotgun at his shoulder and aiming it at Colin.

"Come on now. No need for all this drama," said Revie.

"There is Mr Revie. You have exacerbated a problem we already had. We can't let these patients leave and now we cannot let you leave."

"Why can't we leave?" asked Jonny.

"It will be too dangerous for you," explained Selina, dropping her tone to her conciliatory doctor's vibration.

"It wouldn't be dangerous," said Gwen.

"Would we be arrested?" asked George, who had joined the drama group in the courtyard.

"No, you will not be arrested. I am a Detective Chief Inspector and I will not be arresting you."

"I think we should go with them Doctor and see if we can get home." George looked hopeful and turned to Joseph who stood just behind him. Joseph was folding his arms and staring at Selina.

"Don't believe them. They want to remove you like they did the other patients. They want to split you up and send you to asylums all over the country. This is the only one in north Wales and so you will all be on your way to England." Lloyd Wright was laying it on thick and it was working.

Jonny aimed his gun with more determination and said, "Colin, my old mate, you need to take your friends and go to the cells. They are the most secure, but I will allow you all to be there together. You will be locked in while we decide the best course of action."

Lloyd nodded approval and pointed his gun in the direction he wanted them to go. Gwen was beginning to shake and Colin touched her arm in comfort.

"It's ok. It'll be fine, stop worrying." She smiled and walked on showing no visible sign of fear.

They were soon pushed into the only padded cell which had two beds.

"Sorry pal," said Jonny. "I can't risk going into another asylum where I don't have any mates."

"That won't happen Jonny. I promise that won't happen. Things have moved on now and that just can't happen. I would not lie to you."

Jonny slid the small hatch shut and said, "Can't risk it Colin."

After they had heard the footsteps walking away, Gwen said, "What do we do now boss?"

Revie sat down on one of the beds and thought. "We get out of this cell Gwen and then we get out of this asylum. I'm sorry I doubted you Colin, because I did doubt you. You have knowledge of the way this place works and within that knowledge is our way out of here."

"A quick way out of here," said Gwen. "Apparently I want a wee."

"You will have to wee in that pot," answered Colin, pointing to a bucket -like receptacle in the corner.

"I'll wait a bit," said Gwen.

Thirty minutes later there was a knock at the door and a woman's voice whispered, "Mr Buchanan! It's me, Linda. I've come to help you."

"Linda? That's great, do you have the key?"

"I do Mr Buchanan." They heard the unmistakable turning of a key and soon the door was open. Linda Jones looked really rough, with her partly shaved head and cut about face. She was wringing her sore and chapped hands.

"Will you take me with you Mr Buchanan? I will go straight to confess about killing my parents and trying to kill Darren. I will go to jail and I will take whatever sentence I am given. But whatever you do, please take me away from here. I will die if I have any more of their treatment."

Colin came through the door and held her by the arms.

"Of course you can come with us."

"You two just go up the corridor a bit. I'm going to wee in this pot but I'd rather you weren't listening to me do it."

"Coward," said Revie, but they walked up the corridor anyway.

"I'll wait with you," Linda informed her kindly.

"Thanks," answered Gwen as she piddled away.

Colin and Revie were standing at the far end of the corridor when they returned. They could hear mumbling from the further corridor to their right.

"What's that?" asked Revie.

"That's the men's ward. There are lots of old men in there, you should look Colin," said Linda.

Colin nodded and made his way over. He wagged his fingers at the other two to have a look too. Soon the three were peering through the glass top half of the swing doors. Colin gasped.

"Christ there's been a change in here Linda. Why is everyone so old?"

"They've been getting like that over the past few weeks. There were only one or two at the beginning, while you were here. Didn't you see them?"

"No, no I didn't. I don't think I saw one old person ever. I mean, I thought that was the point? Everyone stayed the same age and got better no matter what injuries they had."

"That was true. If I didn't believe it before, I only have to look at Darren. When I shot him, there was virtually no face left. Now he looks better than before. But something has happened and Dr's Wright and Tresaith are worried, I've heard them talking. I don't know whether it's because some of the patients have been mixing with the intruders or whether it's because the doctors are getting nastier and infecting everyone. Perhaps they have been infected by intruders and that's why they are becoming unhinged? I really couldn't say. I just know I want out and other patients feel the same way."

"Will any of them help us?" asked Revie.

"Some will, others are too scared. But so long as we go now and don't hang around, we can escape."

There was a rise in the sound of chattering as a group appeared to make their way towards them. As they did, there was a loud clattering and rumbling in the men's ward. Gwen put her hand over her mouth to stifle a scream as they saw the men began to climb from their beds and congregate in the centre of the ward. Soon they were walking towards the door and towards the group.

"Move!" said Colin in a hoarse whisper. They did. They scurried down the corridor and Colin pushed them into the library. There they hid behind the door until the group including Selina, Lloyd, Jonny, George and Joseph had passed. Then Colin led the way through the outside door to the courtyard where they trot marched towards the cobbler's shop.

But they were stopped by former patients rushing towards them and forcing them to detour towards the hall. As they ran into the dark building and slammed the door behind, the nurse patients were hammering on the door.

"Oh for fuck's sake. I didn't foresee this when I was having my breakfast," said Gwen as she helped to hold the door shut.

"I don't think you actually have to hold the door shut. The locks look pretty solid and – we can use this wooden bar to reinforce the place." Colin picked up an oak plank and threaded it through the metal supports.

They made their way into the dimly lit hall and sat down on the chairs there. The four took a moment to catch their breath as the hammering appeared to gain momentum. No longer random, the knocking was hitting a rhythm which seemed to change its effect.

"Somethings changed," said Gwen. "I think they can get in now."

They got up and moved along the outside of the hall centre in an effort to find another way out. Linda led them through a side door where they could skip across a short outside alleyway until they reached the offices.

"We should be alright here while we sort out a plan. We know they are over at the hall and in the courtyard," Revie said breathlessly.

"And I expect they will be guarding the cobbler's door to stop us getting out there."

"But Colin, can we leave via the EST room too? Isn't that how you got out before?" Gwen was holding his arm tightly.

"Whether we leave through the EST or the cobbler's, either way we need to create a diversion that will muddy the waters. We need to release all of the patients, especially the single cell ones like Roy." Colin felt in charge but he added. "Is that ok with you, boss?"

Revie nodded. How the fuck could he argue?

CHAPTER TWENTY EIGHT

Colin told Linda to unlock the female wards and tell them to go to the courtyard. He, Revie and Gwen made their swift journey to the locked single cells so that they could release the patients there.

Colin had heard only the odd scream or shout when he spent his five year sabbatical at the asylum, but now there were such chattering and rumblings and terrible noises from everywhere. The noise was sending vibratory tremors down the corridors and through the group. It made them feel sick and shaky and they found it difficult to walk ahead normally. Like the knocking on the hall door, the random screams were merging to create one constant chant which felt as though they could bring down the walls. Lights flickered and blinds flapped and a freezing wind travelled towards them.

"This is a bat shit crazy place Colin," said Revie. "I seriously wish I hadn't come."

"At least we can be sure of having solved a massive case when we get out. All these murderers and rapists and the fraud that's going on with the Tresaiths should get you a DS."

"And what about you two? Do you want to get anything out of it? You don't want to re-join the force do you?"

"Not on your nelly, boss," said Gwen. "I'm thinking of setting up as a private detective, I'm fed up of working in the solicitors office. I thought my degree would have got me a bit further on. This case should get me more clients than I can handle if I advertise it well enough."

"I think I'm going to write a book about it," Colin informed them. He had literally just discovered that he wanted to write a book.

"It seems we all have a lot to gain from sorting this out. So let's get to it. Three intelligent people like us should be able to manage it." Revie smiled. Generally unemotional, Revie could suddenly send out a wave of warmth to his colleagues and they were then prepared to follow him anywhere. Colin and Gwen certainly were.

The first door belonged to Roy Townsend and once unlocked they saw that Roy was standing to attention waiting for them.

"Hello Mr Buchanan. I thought you had managed to escape us for good. Perhaps you can tell me what's going on out there? I've been left alone for over a day now. No food, drink or medicine and all I can hear is screaming and crashing about."

"It's gone a bit pear shaped, I'm afraid, Roy. But my friends and I are in the process of trying to get you all back home but Dr. Tresaith and Dr. Wright don't want you to leave."

"Because if we go they will have to explain what they have been doing with all the money, I suppose."

"I expect it's something like that," answered Colin.

"It is exactly that," said Gwen.

"What do you want me to do?" asked Roy.

"I want you to persuade the others to leave with us and while you are at it, I want you to create a drama which stops the doctors not allowing an escape."

"Sounds like fun. I get to see my kids this way, do I?"

"You do Roy and your wife if you get her out too. She is in Number 22 and the key is hanging up by the light switch."

"You sure about this? I'm not a terribly trustworthy person." But the police group had gone and Roy was talking to himself and free for the first time in years.

Eventually everyone had been unlocked and told to go to the courtyard. It seemed much longer, but the whole job had taken less than 20 minutes. The rhythmic vibration was increasing in noise and each patient released joined in. They all marched through the corridors and streamed towards the yard. Their synchronised marching added to the chanting and the asylum became hotter and hotter.

Colin, Revie and Gwen watched the patients surround Selina and Lloyd who were now standing hand in hand and accompanied by Jonny, George and Joseph.

They all looked terrified.

Colin shouted to them, "We just want to leave here guys. Everyone wants to leave and you can come too with no trouble."

"Leaving here will be nothing but trouble for everyone Colin. Think about it," shouted back Selina.

"Stop trying to scare people Selina. They have a right to finally go home."

"Home doesn't exist for most of you," she cried out. "You have been here for so long that the outside world has completely changed."

"And all your friends and family are dead," added Lloyd.

This announcement did nothing to settle the would - be escapers.

"My children are still alive though, aren't they?" asked Betty, who had been released from her cell and pushed into the throng by Roy.

"Of course the children are still alive," answered Roy. "My boys are tough and they will be building up the business and looking after our interests. And if they aren't doing that, then they know fucking well what I'm going to do to them!" He held a shotgun aloft and fired a cartridge in front of him.

There was a scream and his wife slumped in her wheelchair.

"You've killed her!" shouted Darren.

One of the nurses-cum-patients ran over and checked Betty, "You have killed her. She's dead as she could be."

Gwen went over to Betty and applied her extensive CAS Care knowledge.

"I am afraid that your wife has died Mr Townsend. I am sure that your shot was an accident and you didn't mean to do it, but she is dead."

Roy was still holding the gun and staring at Gwen. Colin watched breathlessly, ready to intervene if necessary. However, he didn't need to because Roy said, "Oh well. She wasn't much of a wife anyway. I'll get me a crazy stripper wife when we leave here. Come on copper, let's get out and into freedom!"

There was a rousing cheer and Roy fired the shotgun again, this time into the air. Revie beckoned to Colin and Gwen and they made their way around the crowd and thought the cobbler's shop door. Colin's last view of the downstairs asylum was a jeering crowd of rapidly aging patients shouting and hurling stones at Selina and Lloyd. They were crouched down with their hands covering their faces and heads and did not see the three of them leave.

"We should help them," said Colin.

"Not here, not now," answered Revie and leant over his friend to close and lock the doors. They heard screaming which thankfully dulled after the doors closed.

"Come on guys, we've got to go and get help. We know how to get in and out now." Gwen was already running.

"We know how to get in," answered Colin and ran after her.

"Can you hear a kind of crackling?" asked Revie as they ran.

"I think it might be Colin's underpants, boss," said Gwen and she grinned at him through her mild hysteria.

"Very funny Gwen. But I can hear it too and it seems way too hot in here," panted Colin. They were all panting because they had all increased their pace in these last hundred metres.

"Unless the patients have set fire to the wards," said Revie.

"And probably the doctors," added Gwen.

"Not our problem," muttered Colin as he unlocked the outside door.

"Bloody hell," he said. "This handle is hot."

"Be careful!" shouted Revie.

"Because the fire might be outside?" said Colin.

Gwen was on her phone, "I've got a signal, and I'm calling it in."

"Gwen, you're not Police anymore, I'll call it in." Revie took the phone from Gwen's hand and dialled.

"Twat," Colin said to Gwen.

She wasn't embarrassed in the least. "I've been acting like police all day today so I forgot. Plus I had to wee in a bucket and I am entitled to be a twat."

They giggled like schoolchildren until Revie finished his call.

"Apparently the asylum is on fire and there is one engine already here and more coming from other stations. The new security lot saw it and now everything is on its way."

"Do they know where we are?" asked Gwen. She was mainly interested in whether they knew how to get them out. Hopefully there was not some kind of double spooky lock system that prevented anyone getting in and out.

No – this wasn't a Joseph Glanvill tale.

"They do and they are coming straight to the door. They are worried that if we open it from here there will be a flashback and we will die a horrible, horrible death."

"Like in Towering Inferno?"

"Well I'm no Fred Astaire," said Revie.

"Ginger Rogers?" asked Colin.

"I don't think she was in it…"

Their intelligent conversation was interrupted by the sound of sirens and engines. It took another fifteen minutes before the doors were opened to reveal several fire officers standing in the blackened and smouldering area surrounding the doorway.

"DCI Revie?" asked one. "Aaaah and your colleagues are with you. That's good. Is there anyone else we need to rescue?"

Before he could be answered, the sound of running boots on corridors and loud screaming came nearer.

"What the hell is that?" asked the inquisitive fireman.

"That's a hell of a lot of paperwork making its way towards us," said Revie and jumped out of the doorway with Colin and Gwen closely following.

Revie marched straight over to ACC Ryan whom he saw talking to several uniforms on the open driveway. As he made it into a clearer view he became aware of just how much of the asylum was actually on fire. Huge flames reached into the sky from every rooftop and the broken windows and doorways shone yellow and red with the raging fire that burned within the walls.

"Christ sir. What's happened here?"

"Arson. The usual, vandals messing around and starting fires. We only found out about your visit here when you telephoned. You should have let us know."

"If you check with Sally, she should have told you." Sally the DC who had been helping him out was less than useful and Revie would be glad when she moved on.

"DC Jones is off sick, today John. She didn't tell us anything. Now I need you to bring me up to speed with this nonsense."

Revie was as brief as he possibly could be and was not interrupted until he finished.

"So, is that who that lot are?"

DS Thomas pointed at the 30 or so bedraggled men and women who were standing on the yard, silhouetted against the burning buildings.

CHAPTER TWENTY NINE

"You need to get those people medical treatment and above all you need to make sure they don't escape. Amongst the ill ones are some serious criminals and Roy Townsend – him there – may have a shotgun."

Revie walked over to Colin and Gwen, both of whom were leaning against one of the police cars.

"They are bringing more officers and ambulances. This is a major incident and it's only going to get more complicated once they go downstairs."

"Major incident now but they didn't believe me when I told them about it," sulked Colin.

"Don't be a mard arse Colin. You will be famous from now on and I bet you get fed up of it before the media does."

Colin digested this thought. "Ok boss. What should we do now?"

Revie was saved from answering when some screaming and shouting which overtopped the rest of the screaming and shouting, rang clearly in their direction.

"Mr Buchanan! You promised you would help me! You promised!" It was Linda Jones, kneeling on the wet grass and banging the ground with her fists.

Colin walked over, closely followed by Gwen and put his hand on her shoulder. She shrugged this off and stared at him.

"You said you would help me. What is happening?" Colin stared at her battered face and body. She looked worse now with the hose water and falling soot covering her meagre clothes. She was scarred and scared and began to whimper.

"The paramedics will be with you soon, Linda. They will help you." Suddenly, Colin was pushed aside roughly and Darren appeared in front of them. Darren's face was changing and deteriorating so rapidly that they were mesmerised with the flesh as it peeled and fell to the ground. Colin thought that the scorching on Darren's chest was due to the fire but soon realised that it was shotgun residue. He was reverting to the Darren he had been - should have been.

"You fucking bitch Linda. I'm supposed to forgive you but I can't. You killed your parents and then tried to kill me. I will go to court to make sure you get properly punished."

"You will go down too Darren. You were in on it and I will tell the police how much you were involved."

Revie joined them and said, "You will all be giving statements and evidence as necessary. But in the meantime we need to get this lot sorted out."

A couple more paramedics took charge and the three of them moved away.

"They are still coming out," Revie informed them.

"Any sign of Lloyd and Selina?" asked Gwen.

"Not yet, unless of course they left by another door. But they tell me that would be difficult because the whole place is firmly on fire and is surrounded by fire and police and if anyone did escape – they would likely be well alight."

"You paint a pretty picture boss," answered Colin. "Are we going back in?"

"We aren't. But I believe some unit will, just as soon as the fire is out and the place made safe. No one is going to send their people into a fire in an unsafe building."

"But there are so many people still down there," cried Gwen.

More shouting came from behind them and they saw some of the Tresaith family arguing with one of the uniforms.

"You can't come any further in Mr Tresaith," said Revie as he made his way towards them. They were by the gate which led to Tresaith Manor.

"This is my building and I demand to come through. Is anyone hurt?"

Carys Tresaith moved in front of her uncle and was looking startled. "Who are all of those people Mr Revie? They look old and sort of weird. Is everyone alright?"

Revie smiled at her and said kindly, "Most are Miss Tresaith, but it is a very confusing incident here and I think that you should go home." He straightened up. "I suggest you go home Mr Tresaith. I will come and see you as soon as I can, we have lots to talk about I am sure you can appreciate."

He nodded and said, "I have no idea who all those people are Inspector Revie, they are nothing to do with the family."

"Chef Inspector Revie," he corrected him. "Now please go home and perhaps you might like to speak to your solicitor."

Carys looked at her uncle quizzically and took his hand to lead him away.

The fire was rapidly increasing in volume. Parts of the asylum were crashing down and the great old stones rolling towards the crowds. The order was swiftly given to remove everyone from the scene to various boundaries, dependent upon their current role at the incident. The patients were moved away in unmarked ambulances to an undisclosed location, for now the media were arriving in their vans and their satellite trucks.

"Not a word about any of this to anyone," had been the instruction given to all personnel present. "Leave us to talk to the press."

The fire raged for another twelve hours and even then it only quietened down as its food supply diminished. The old building, the much loved and iconic symbol of Tresaith was being reduced to a pile of rubble and would never stand again. The press and the locals were informed that it could not be confirmed, but early indications were arson. The stories ran away with examples and discussion of vandals and trespassers and the selfish attitude of ghost hunters and the like.

It was three days later before the relevant personnel were able to enter the site. They climbed over the now crumpled stonework and through piles of broken woodwork and glass. There was no part left which inferred a Gothic building of any description. Under instruction, they headed to the place where they had been informed the cobbler's shop was. In the courtyard was a collapsed grand hall surrounded by satellites of stone heaps, any one of which could have been a cobbler's shop. The doorway on the southern side through which the old patients and coppers ex and current had exited was not there. Neither was the building to which the doors had been attached. Another smouldering mass of stone and wood lay in its place.

A JCB with the words Gwyn Howson painted along its arm was brought in and in spite of moving a mountain of rubble, nothing was uncovered. There was no evidence of bodies or occupied hospital rooms or secret passages.

DCI Revie took statements from the Tresaith family in the company of their solicitor who challenged him to discover any financial irregularities or proof of secret patients.

"Do not besmirch our name in order to hide your mental aberrations, Mr Revie," was one of the poetic statements from John Tresaith.

Revie was unfazed by this threat as he knew he had at least 30 ex-patients who could give evidence against them.

On this matter though, he had reached a brick wall. He could find only three patients, Roy Townsend, Linda Jones and her cousin Darren, who were all being treated at a military facility on Anglesey. When Revie enquired of his ACC where the rest of them were, he was told to accompany him to a lab at the facility. Once there, they looked through a large window which only became transparent at a command from one of the officers. On a table in the centre of a room were twenty odd boxes. The lid was taken from one by a woman dressed in a biohazard suit and the box she leant towards the window. It contained ashes.

"Those are your patients," said the ACC.

"They've been cremated?"

"No. They turned to ash in their beds. Just disintegrated and turned to ash in the style of a Peter Cushing horror film."

The window returned to a mirror and the policemen walked away.

"How are we going to present this as a case?"

"John, we won't be presenting it anywhere. This case has gone further up the food chain and we are out."

"That's not right sir! There is too much at stake. I'm going to resign over this if something isn't done.

"Well resign if you must, it won't do any good. You haven't heard this from me, but I believe that John Tresaith knows something about a couple of politicians and a couple of high up spooks. Maybe they have placed members of their family in the asylum. Who knows? Who cares? Buchanan will be getting a damn good pay out and Hughes will too if they keep their mouths shut. You can choose a pay out now or a ridiculous pension and a transfer to Yorkshire. What's it to be?"

CHAPTER THIRTY

Two years had passed and life was going on in Tresaith much as it had before.

John Tresaith was negotiating with the council, many of whom were his friends, about the possible development of the asylum site. Some of the discussions were around the reuse of the stone in the new houses or whether it should be sold. There was more interest than there should have been in the asylum rubble, to the point where John Tresaith appointed the now recovered Selwyn as a commission earning sales man at the site.

Selwyn was in his element in the role. He quickly discovered that he was able to sell each stone or melted metal fragment for stupid amounts of money. Many of his customers were the same people he had thrown out as trespassers over the years. They knew what they wanted and often came back again and again with a truck or lorry or just a trailer as they completed their folly builds back home. Tresaith had been offered a large sum for the whole lot, but it seemed he did not want anyone there whom he was unable to control.

"It's not as though we need the money," he said to Selwyn one day.

"No sir. And this way the site will cleared without any more interfering," said Selwyn.

"Yes indeed. That's what we want. Let me know if there is anything you think I ought to know."

"Of course sir."

John Tresaith continued as he always did, caring only about himself and the family name. He used his well-connected friends in whatever way was deemed necessary to benefit him. They were all rich, why should they care?

*

When the Townsend family discovered that their father was out and their mother dead, there was very little celebration.

"I don't want him back here interfering and causing trouble," said Stephen.

"John Tresaith isn't going to make anything public about the payments and so we are safe," added Gary.

Andrew joined in. "So we should get him into a home as soon as possible and then we are free."

"And all we have to do is inject him with this?" Gary held up a box containing a syringe and a phial.

"John Tresaith said it would work. I'm pissed off with Dad constantly telling us what he's going to turn round and very nearly do…"

"If we are all agreed, I will go and do it now. No need to involve anyone else, especially Barbara, she asks too many questions as it is." Gary packed the box up.

"And we save money. John said he won't last many weeks after this injection," said Stephen.

"Home and free," grinned Andrew.

*

Linda and Darren didn't make it beyond three weeks. Darren's face almost dissolved and he was put on a life support for the last two weeks of his life. His sobbing mother agreed to turn off the machine and after the funeral drove over to Grange Farm and set fire to it. This helped no one, as Grange Farm had been sold not long after the asylum fire unbeknownst to her and was now in the ownership of an equestrian family from Cheshire. They managed to save their animals but were forced to live in a caravan while the insurance company sorted out their problems. She lit the fire because she was not able to set fire to Linda, she having died two days after being rescued from the asylum.

The story put about by the authorities was that these three had been hiding in the asylum and the old nurses' home for years, creating dramas for the ghost hunters and vandals. It had been easy for them when the hospital was first closed and they hadn't gone on to their proper transfer destinations. There had been food and beds and medicine and their hiding place became more unfriendly the longer they were there. Their motive for this unlikely stunt was supposed to be that they did not want to leave Tresaith Asylum and their collective madness had made them stay there. No wonder there were constant reports from Selwyn about intruders. Perhaps it was one of the three who had burnt the place to the ground while lighting a fire. Then, injured and weak they had been unable to put it out.

Utter bollocks was Selwyn's opinion on this version of events. But then Selwyn often had strong opinions and so was not listened to too closely.

Another theory was that one of the ghost hunters had inadvertently or deliberately started a fire under instructions from the Tresaiths.

"It's a good way to get planning pushed through for houses without any restrictions," said one.

"They had no chance with the listed building status on it," agreed another.

There was plenty of gossip and no follow ups.

*

Colin met Psychic Dave and Sarah in The Dog at Tresaith one Wednesday evening. They had been particularly nervous to meet the ex-policeman and had taken quite a bit of persuading. They told Colin why after he had bought the first round of drinks.

"We got visited by the Men in Black," Dave informed them.

"Will Smith?" asked Colin.

"No, our equivalent. They told us that if we posted those pictures anywhere again, we would find it very difficult to find work, get credit, and get a passport or driving licence and all that. I told them to sod off, but I was scared, really scared. They brought up the fact there have been a few little indiscretions on my police record. You know, a bit of drugs and some demos and they said they would make sure I would disappear for a very long time. And Dave here, well he's had that problem in the loos in Winsford Flashes about 20 years ago and they said that they would make sure the press got hold of it. Didn't they Dave?"

"Yes and I've got a wife and kids and a job at the bank now. I mean, I've heard about this sort of thing happening, but I didn't think that it actually would."

"And who is going to believe us? You try telling someone that MI5 or someone had visited and threatened you, especially because they think we are conspiracy theorists anyway."

Colin listened intently. He was researching for the book he was going to write about their experiences at Tresaith. He was changing names in order to cover his back but had still been surprised how many people told him about these visits. He had asked Revie for his opinions even though he was now based in Yorkshire and involved in murder cases there.

"I'll help you with a bit of background, but I suggest you do not identify me, quote me nor use me in your book. This is higher than both of us."

"I'm not going to write a factual book. I'm writing fiction but that's because no one will believe it as truth. I just wanted to know why people are being shut down."

"They'll shut you down too Colin. Be careful. There are some very important names involved and that should be enough. They had family members down there too and they aren't going to allow you to reveal that, are you? It always been this way, you know how the world really works. Twas ever thus."

"Do you still have the picture?" he asked Sarah.

"I do, but you can't show it anywhere. We are probably in enough trouble just talking to you."

"I won't use it in the book and I won't name you at all. It's going to be a work of fiction - it's for my own curiosity really. "

Sarah took her tablet from her bag and searched through her pictures. "That's you," she said.

The picture was indistinct and Colin might have said that it was a badly Photo Shopped image of him. Trouble was that he knew full well he had been standing on the other side of that clock tower window when Sarah was taking the snaps.

"Can I keep these?" he asked. "I won't use them."

"I can give you all the raw footage and pictures I have of the place. There's a lot." She handed him several USB sticks.

"Are you sure? I probably won't need all of them."

"They are less likely to kill you than us. I want someone to keep a record," Sarah said, biting her nails.

"Come on Sarah, let's go." Dave got him from his chair and took Sarah's arm. Colin smiled and thanked them and noticed how subdued the pair were when they passed his window on Vale Street outside the pub.

He rang Gwen.

"Hey. I've just had a weird meeting with Sarah and Dave and now I'm going to have a last look at the site before I come home."

"All your meetings have been weird since you decided to do this. Still think it's a good idea?"

"I do. Someone has to tell the real story, even disguised as fiction."

"No one is going to believe it's real."

"I know. Oh, I've come up with a title."

"Go on."

"Glyndwr Hospital."

"I'm not convinced. I'll let you know."

The call finished and Colin leant back to finish his drink. Tresaith was a funny old place and he would be glad to leave it. He was sure that the drinkers were looking at him as though he was someone who was here to cause trouble, but perhaps that was just his fancy. He and Gwen were now an item and both had sold their houses and moved to Nefyn where Gwen had family. He owned a fuck off big house and car and lived off his large pension and settlement. The idea of the book had burned in his brain and his therapist told him it would be a good way to rid himself of his demons.

Since then he had interviewed the Dr. Poole, whose father had worked at the asylum and between them, they realised that the Colin Watson who worked at the asylum was in fact Colin's grandfather. The ledger he had taken from the asylum told him a lot about Watson's involvement and Colin wasn't sure that he wanted to make that public. Colin wanted to follow up on that angle but was hitting a brick wall in respect of his family giving him access to Dr. Watson's records. It appeared to be something to do with the court case and eviction notice on his granddaughter Alice. Small world revolving, Colin had thought.

He knew that the Tresaith family and their connections had prevented any enquiry and hadn't realised how possible that actually was until he had been involved in it. His research had turned up nothing on Selina and Lloyd and he couldn't be sure whether they had escaped or been burned along with the other patients. There was also the alarming possibility that they were still underground or in the parallel universe or whatever it was and trapped again. But he had no intention of going back there to check.

And so far he hadn't discovered who had started the fire.

He left the pub and walked up the steep hill to the market place. Shoppers were out in the sunshine and the town was busy. He was in deep thought when someone prodded him in the back and made him jump. He swung round to see Carys Tresaith. She was quite the young lady.

"Hello Mr Buchanan. I've just been to the hairdressers." She pointed to a beauty and hair salon frequented by many in town.

"Well you look lovely." He stopped because he couldn't remember whether he was allowed to give compliments to young women or whether it was considered inappropriate.

"Thank you. I try."

"What are you up to Carys?"

"Walking home, do you want to come with me?"

"I'm parked over there, but yes I was going to have a quick look at the asylum before I leave. I'm writing a book and just back here for some research."

"Have you spoken to my family at all?"

"No. I guessed that they wouldn't speak to me."

"I think you are correct. They won't speak to you. But I will."

Colin turned to her and asked, "Do you have something to tell me?"

"I can tell you about a dream I had. Shall I?"

"If you like." Colin was conscious that they were walking towards Love Lane which was a short cut to the hospital. This was a lonely lane and he didn't fancy taking a 14 year old, or was she 15? He wasn't going to be on his own with her up a lonely lane anyway.

"Let's sit here," he said, pointing to a bench by the Butter Market.

She grinned as though guessing why he had said that. Sitting down she handed him a piece of chocolate which he refused. Tresaithians walked from shop to shop and across the road. This was a busy little town he thought.

"Now, we are comfortable and safely in full view of the whole town, I will tell you about my dream. You know that Selina and Lloyd were my parents. I knew that Selina was my mother for years even though she left me at the manor with my uncles. But I only discovered that Lloyd Wright was my father when he got in touch with me and told me."

"Is this the dream or real now?"

"This part is real. Selina was working in Canada I was told and would come back when she could. She was doing some important work in a hospital there which I believed when I was younger but realised it sounded wrong as I got older. Then Lloyd turned up one day and told me that my uncles wouldn't let me see him and I knew that was likely to be true. He would visit me and chat with me online and I really got to love him and trust him. He's such a great person and told me that as soon as I had finished school and was old enough he would take me to Canada and the Tresaiths couldn't do a damn thing about it. He told me about the life we would have together, just him and me. Oh I loved him, but of course now he is dead."

"I'm sorry about that. It must be difficult for you."

"Hmmm - and now the dream part. I dreamt that Lloyd came to Tresaith on one of his secret visits and we met in the woods and he told me how well the plans were going at the new house he was building in Canada. He showed me pictures and I was so happy. Then he left me when the thunderstorm started and instead of going back home, this time I decided to follow him. He went to the asylum and I couldn't understand that but I followed him anyway. He walked there and went into one of the airing yards and then I saw you come out and you and he go back in. I saw some of those ghost hunters and the caretaker and his darling dog. I decided to follow Lloyd inside."

Colin was shifting uncomfortably because this was difficult to listen to.

"So I went inside and kept myself hidden and saw Selina torturing some poor woman who was covered in blood and she was crying. You looked ill and then you left. I was going to follow you out, but I thought I should stay. Lloyd didn't seem bothered about the torture and then they both left that room and were talking and laughing then arguing and then eventually Selina took him to a room where he went in. Selina walked off and so I decided to follow Lloyd and see what he was up to. And ohhh – Mr Buchanan it was horrible. He was with this woman and he took her clothes off and he took his clothes off and then he was doing things to her that animals don't do. I've seen those kinds of films at school when Felicity Broadgate brought some in and I couldn't believe that Lloyd was doing it! Then they stopped and fell asleep and then Selina came back and they argued and left. Then I saw this woman and she was really old like a horror film and Lloyd had been doing things to her. He had promised that he only loved me and would only cuddle me." She was genuinely crying now.

"What happened next?" He was almost too frightened to hear.

"I ran out and went home and wouldn't go outside and was crying and angry all the time. Uncle John and Uncle Philip didn't know what to do with me. Then after a while my crying stopped and I was just so angry that I went back. Then I saw you and a woman and that Inspector go in and I followed you. You are all rubbish because none of you ever saw me. But I saw you get caught and put in those cells so I went to the tortured woman and gave her the keys I had picked up from the floor when the other patient dropped them and told her to help you. I think she thought I was a ghost or something. Anyway then I saw how Selina and Lloyd were behaving and came out again."

"Did you see who started the fire?"

"I'm only telling you my dream, Mr Buchanan. It's not real. But, in the dream I lit the fire. I lit fires everywhere and before long it was all alight. I hate Tresaith Asylum and I wanted it to die. Then I phoned 999 and just watched until Uncle John came."

"And this was all a dream?" She turned to him and in her eyes Colin noticed a coldness she had hidden very well to that point. He had seen the same look in the eyes of Selina.

"A dream yes. And if you tell anyone I said any different, I shall come to your house and burn that down too. Goodbye Mr Buchanan. Have a nice life."

She got up, put in her earphones and walked up Love Lane.

Colin didn't get up from the bench for a while.

He couldn't.